The Magnolias Of Atherton Hall

GARY ROWE

Copyright © 2018 Gary Rowe

Printed in the United States of America

All rights reserved. No part of this publication can be reproduced, distributed, or transmitted in any form or by any means, or stored in a database or retrieval system, without the prior written permission of the publisher and author, Gary Rowe.

ISBN-10: 1979667934
ISBN-13: 978-1979667937

Cover Painting © 2018
by Vivien Willis
Inspired by Thomas Gainsborough's "The Morning Walk"

The characters and events in this book are fictitious. Any similarity to real persons, living or dead, is coincidental and not intended by the author.

DEDICATION

THIS BOOK IS DEDICATED to the memory of my father, Bill. Dad was so proud of my writing but he unfortunately passed before having the opportunity to read my first novel, *Echoes From Sandcastle Heights*. Like the subject of this novel, his love of nature will always be part of me.

ACKNOWLEDGMENTS

A SPECIAL THANK YOU to my dear friend, Vivien Willis, who painted another impressive piece of art for the cover of this book. She beautifully brought the main characters to life.

THE MAGNOLIAS OF ATHERTON HALL

Charles Town, South Carolina

Early June, 1765

GARY ROWE

Chapter 1

"It won't be long, little one!," Lawrence Eldridge said to his nine-year-old daughter as she leaned against the railing of the ship's deck.

Sarah Eldridge intently watched the busy dock from the deck of the ship as it slowly sailed into the Charles Town harbor. The mid-day sun, shining brightly over the town, glistened off the water while the brilliant beams of light from the sky caused Sarah's mother, Caroline, to adjust her own hat to shield her eyes from the glaring sun. As Sarah stood between her parents, raising herself up on the tips of her toes, her blonde curls fell forward as she leaned over the rail to get an even better downward view. Sarah's blue eyes widened with excitement as she eagerly watched the workers quickly move along the dock as they carried trunks from arriving ships and loaded them onto waiting carriages. By the sight of this familiar scene, Sarah knew they had almost reached their destination.

"Do you think they will be in full bloom?," Sarah excitedly asked her parents.

"It is that time of year!," her mother replied, knowing exactly what Sarah meant.

"I can't wait to smell that wonderful scent!," Sarah exclaimed.

Three days earlier, Sarah and her parents boarded the ship in the Virginia Colony to embark on their annual sojourn. Each year in early June they would travel from their home in Williamsburg to visit her father's sister Lavinia, her husband George Lockwood and their daughter Lucinda at their South Carolina plantation.

"Ahoy!," a familiar voice called from the dock below and waved at the Eldridges standing on the deck of the ship.

"Uncle George!," Sarah called out with excitement as she and her parents returned his wave.

When Sarah and her parents finally debarked the ship and walked along the wooden plank to reach the dock, thoughts of Sarah's first visit a few years earlier began to enter her mind. She never could have imagined how that initial trip would make such a lasting impression. As Sarah recalled her first encounter with that exhilarating scent and the beautiful white petals of the large luscious blossoms set against the dark green leaves of the magnificent magnolia tree, an expression of sheer delight could be seen in the smile that appeared between her rosy cheeks.

"It's so good to see you all!," George Lockwood called out, interrupting Sarah's thoughts as he suddenly appeared from behind a few crates stacked on the dock. "I'm glad to see you all had a safe journey!," he added.

"Hello, dear brother-in-law!," Caroline said as she stepped off the plank and onto the dock.

"Lavinia has been looking forward to your visit!," George said as Caroline gave him a hug.

"How is my dear sister?," Lawrence asked his brother-in-law as they shook hands.

"She has been counting the days until your arrival!," George replied. "Hello, Sarah! Lucinda has been anxious to see you too!," George continued as he gave his niece a quick hug.

"I can't wait to see her too!," Sarah eagerly replied as she watched two men loading their trunks onto the back of the familiar carriage.

"Your carriage awaits!," George invitingly said to his guests as he raised his hand in the direction of the regal looking white carriage with its black leather seats.

"Are the magnolias in bloom?," Sarah asked her uncle with excitement as everyone walked toward the carriage.

"They certainly are! They bloomed because they knew you were coming!," George teased his niece as he stepped aside for the two ladies to board.

"Oh, Uncle George!," Sarah exclaimed as she laughed at her uncle's sense of humor while Lawrence lifted her up to place her on the rear seat and then focused his attention on Caroline.

Once Caroline and Sarah were comfortably situated inside and the trunks secured at the rear, George and Lawrence climbed up into the driver seat as George took the reins of the shiny black thoroughbreds who would lead the carriage onto the main road. After Caroline raised her parasol to shield herself and Sarah from the bright sun, the horses eagerly moved ahead as George drove them at a slow gait through the center of the town. The dusty road bustled with traffic from the other carriages while pedestrians occasionally walked in front of them as they crossed the street. "Steady on," George cooed to his horses after a child darted in front of another carriage startling its driver and horses. Sarah suddenly tensed as she witnessed the event but afterwards visibly relaxed knowing they were safe in the hands of Uncle George.

"Look, mother! See all the new houses!," Sarah exclaimed as she realized the scene was different from their previous visit.

"Yes, Sarah, I have been noticing that as well! It seems every year we visit the town has grown a little more," Caroline replied.

As the powerful black horses pulled the carriage ahead on the roadway, the town began to fade as they continued to their journey's end. Sarah could hardly contain her excitement of what she knew would lie ahead once the carriage approached the grand old house called Magnolia Grove.

Sarah always enjoyed seeing the river town but her heart belonged to Virginia and the colonial capital she knew so well. Williamsburg had been her home all of her life. However, Williamsburg also held a special place in her parents' hearts since that is where their story began.

Lawrence Eldridge, Sarah's father, who was the youngest son of a wealthy Virginia planter family, knew he would not inherit the family plantation. He had no complaints about his station in life because he understood the English customs that had been carried down for generations that required the eldest male to inherit the bulk of the family holdings. His eldest brother, Thomas, would inherit the family land and its legacy. Penderley, the Eldridge's plantation, was located on the James River in Charles City County. The 12,000-acre estate was developed by Lawrence's father, Nathaniel, after receiving a land grant from King George I of England in the late 1720s. Over the decades it thrived as a successful plantation harvesting tobacco, other crops and livestock.

After arriving in America, Nathaniel Eldridge and his new bride, Abigail Pendleton, soon built a brick mansion on Nathaniel's newly gifted land. Nathaniel received this grant because his father, Jeremiah, who was under the command of the younger General Robert Atherton, had been a strong force in the development of Britain's Royal Regiment of Artillery in the early 1700s. King George I intended to reward Jeremiah for his dedication to the British Crown. However, Jeremiah passed away before being presented with the honor. Therefore, the King presented a land grant in the Virginia Colony to his son Nathaniel to ensure Jeremiah's efforts were rewarded.

Nathaniel Eldridge's wife Abigail, who was also born in England, was a member of the wealthy Pendleton family from the County of Kent in South East England. With their fortunate circumstances, Nathaniel and his bride sailed across the Atlantic Ocean to begin their new life together in the English colony. Their hard work and determination to create a prosperous life in America was soon fulfilled when Nathaniel began to focus on the cultivation of tobacco. The prosperous crop soon brought additional wealth and status for his growing family. Nathaniel and Abigail's union produced two sons and a daughter. Thomas, being the eldest, knew from an early age the duty and responsibility that was bestowed upon him to preserve his family's heritage. Lawrence was also groomed with the knowledge of running a successful plantation in the event that Thomas could not fulfill his duty due to any unfortunate circumstances. Nathaniel felt his family was complete when Abigail gave birth to a daughter who they named Lavinia.

Lawrence took great pride in working with his father and brother to ensure the success of the plantation. However, he felt something was missing in his life. When he expressed his desires to his father to study law, Nathaniel encouraged Lawrence to attend the College of William and Mary in nearby Williamsburg. Nathaniel was delighted with the idea since he felt that a legal profession would not only benefit his son, but would also benefit the family business when the burden of a legal matter presented itself.

Not long after Lawrence's arrival in the capital city, he befriended a fellow student from the South Carolina Colony who had been sent to the college by his family to be educated. Lawrence soon learned that his new friend, George Lockwood, was from a well-known family similar to his own in both background and status. While Lawrence's father successfully grew tobacco, George's family was triumphant in the cultivation of rice. George was being groomed to inherit his family's legacy but his father felt that George would have the ability to be more successful if educated and hoped that his newly acquired knowledge would be beneficial to running a successful plantation.

During their first break from school, Lawrence invited George to return to Penderley during their time away from school and to introduce him to his family. Upon his introduction to Lawrence's younger sister, George fell madly in love with Lavinia. George frequently returned with Lawrence to Penderley on every opportunity that presented itself and a deep love developed between him and Lavinia.

In addition to befriending George, Lawrence soon met the beautiful Caroline Hemsworth. While attending a local dance held at Raleigh Tavern, Lawrence was introduced by a watchful father to his lovely and well-mannered daughter who immediately captivated his heart. Caroline's father, Joshua, was well aware of the Eldridge's status and had no opposition to Lawrence's interest in his daughter even though she was eight years his junior. He admired Lawrence's ambition and knew he couldn't ask for a more well-suited match for his daughter. Joshua, being a well-respected man in his own right, was a well-known resident, contractor and surveyor and had also been educated at the college as a young man. After graduating nearly two decades earlier, Joshua established himself in Williamsburg and became known as a respectable contractor. His honest reputation led him to becoming one of the contractors that oversaw the addition of the ballroom that was added to the rear of the Governor's Palace in 1752.

A few years prior, in the early 1740s, Joshua had built his home after choosing a lot on Palace Street facing the Palace Green. He felt the location was a prestigious one since it was closely situated near the Governor's Palace. The Georgian-style home he built, Hemsworth House, became known as one of the handsomest houses in Williamsburg. During the construction, Caroline's mother Catherine suddenly died. Joshua, along with the help of Catherine's mother, raised Caroline. Joshua loved his daughter dearly and after Lawrence asked Caroline for her hand in marriage, Joshua bequeathed the house to his daughter and new son-in-law as a wedding present. Joshua remained with them until his untimely death when Sarah was only four years old.

Once Lawrence and George graduated from the college, Lawrence soon established himself as an honest and respectable lawyer in Williamsburg. His success eventually led to his appointment as a judge in the capital city at the young age of forty. Lawrence, in his elder years, became a professor of law at the College of William Mary.

After a whirlwind courtship, George asked for Lavinia's hand in marriage and the two were married at Penderley before she returned with him to South Carolina. Over the years, the two couples developed an unbreakable bond that led to Lawrence and Caroline's annual trip to Magnolia Grove Plantation.

As the open carriage continued on its path and eventually to the curve of the last bend in the road, Sarah's excitement grew as she saw the towering trees dotted with the large white blooms she had come to love so well.

"Look, mother!," Sarah pointed. "We are almost there!," she continued as Lawrence leaned to his side and looked back to see the beautiful blue eyes of his daughter widen with excitement.

Set among the trees in the distance, the Lockwood's stately white-columned mansion gleamed as the sunlight reflected off its white-washed brick walls. As the carriage drew closer and the view became clearer, the powerful lemony scent that had become so vivid in Sarah's memory suddenly filled the air and overtook her senses. When the carriage turned off the main road and drove through the brick-columned pillars and under the magnolia trees that graced the entrance, Sarah glanced upward in amazement at the limbs of the tall trees and the rich green leaves that surrounded the large luscious white flowers.

"I told you they had bloomed just for you!," George once again teased his niece as he saw the excitement on her face.

"I'm so glad they did!," Sarah responded with glee as she giggled over her words.

"I'm sure you all will be glad to get settled after your long journey," George said as he turned to look at Lawrence and Caroline as the carriage made its way down the pathway across the expansive front lawn.

When the carriage came to the end of the pathway and followed the circular loop in front of the house, Lavinia and Lucinda appeared from the large wood-paneled entrance door and walked onto the wide veranda underneath the huge white columns to greet their guests.

"Welcome to Magnolia Grove!," Lavinia exclaimed while George brought the horses to a halt in front of the steps and began to climb down from the carriage.

"We have been so looking forward to our visit!," Caroline said to her sister-in-law after Lawrence had climbed down from the driver seat to help her exit the carriage. "Hello, Lucinda! It is so nice to see you!," she said to her smiling niece who was standing on the veranda beside her mother.

"Hello, Sarah!," Lucinda called out to Sarah as Sarah raced up the steps to greet her after Lawrence had lifted her up from the carriage seat to place her safely down to the ground.

"Hello, cousin Lucinda!," Sarah replied as she fell into her cousin's arms.

"Please, come into the house and let's get you settled," Lavinia said to Caroline and Lawrence as they stood beside George next to the carriage.

"I'll have your trunks delivered to your rooms," George said as he motioned to the house servants who were waiting a short distance away for George's instructions. "Thank you, Ezra and Zach," George continued as the servants moved to the rear of the carriage to perform their assigned task.

"Yes, Master George," Ezra replied as George stepped aside to allow Caroline and Lawrence to climb the steps.

"It is so nice to be here!," Caroline said as she reached to give Lavinia a hug once everyone had joined her on the veranda.

"How is my favorite sister?," Lawrence teased as he kissed his sister on the cheek.

"I would take that as a compliment if I wasn't your only sister," Lavinia replied while laughing at her brother's humor.

"You would still be my favorite if you weren't!," Lawrence continued to tease as he laughed along with her.

"How do you put up with him?," Lavinia jested as she turned to smile at Caroline.

"He can be a handful sometimes! But he is still my knight in shining armor," Caroline said as the four adults laughed.

"You are my knight in shining armor too!," Lavinia said as she looked lovingly at her husband to include him in the conversation.

"Thank you, dear," George replied as he returned his wife's playfulness.

"Please, come into the house," Lavinia said as she led the way to the front door while returning her attention toward making her guests feel at home. "After you all have recuperated from your journey, I thought we would relax on the veranda with some refreshment," Lavinia suggested as she and George ushered everyone into the front hall.

"That would be lovely!," Caroline replied while everyone gathered at the foot of the stairs.

While everyone stood in the spacious hall, Caroline took a few seconds to silently admire the feeling of grandeur she always felt when entering the entrance hall at Magnolia Grove. The beautiful oil paintings that graced the walls, elegant wall paper and rich mahogany furniture set within the high ceilings and classic architectural details provided an opulent feeling unlike she and Lawrence's more modest home.

"Ezra and Zach will be up shortly with your trunks," George informed as he headed toward the front door to oversee the task. "I'll see you all when you come back down," he continued.

"I'll walk with you to your rooms to make sure everything is okay," Lavinia said as she led them up the wide staircase.

"Sarah, let me show you my new doll I have in my room!," Lucinda said as she suddenly interjected the conversation.

"Yes!," Sarah replied with excitement.

"I'll race you up the stairs!," Lucinda challenged Sarah as they both giggled while passing the adults on the steps in a whirlwind as they darted up the stairs.

After Lavinia had escorted her family down the upstairs corridor to their rooms, she discreetly scanned her surroundings to make sure that the servants had prepared everything just as she had requested. Once she realized she was pleased with what she saw, Lavinia turned toward the doorway to leave her guests.

"Once you all are rested, come down at your leisure," Lavinia said as she left them to refresh themselves after their long journey.

GARY ROWE

Chapter 2

"Thank you, Sibby," Lavinia said to the young servant as she walked onto the veranda and placed the serving tray on the table. "I'll pour the tea if you will serve Mr. Lockwood and Judge Eldridge their beer," Lavinia instructed. "I'll tend to serving the cakes," she continued.

"Yes, ma'am," Sibby replied to her mistress while glancing at the delectable treats resting on the bone china plate.

"Thank you," Lawrence said to Sibby with a smile as he reached out to take the cool beverage.

"That will be all for now," Lavinia said once Sibby had served the men.

The soft afternoon breeze carried the rich scent of magnolias through the air as the four adults comfortably reclined on the veranda while enjoying their refreshments. As they watched the two young girls playing on the front lawn under the magnolia trees, Caroline said to Lavinia, "They do grow up so fast, don't they?"

"Yes, they do. If only time could stand still. At least for a while," Lavinia fondly replied to her sister-in-law as she poured both of them a cup of tea.

"Due to the current political situation that may not be a good idea," George jokingly said to Lavinia's response to Caroline.

"Oh, no! Not politics again!," Lavinia said as she playfully rolled her eyes.

"Don't deprive us men of a little enjoyment," George teased.

"Speaking of politics, I heard that South Carolina fared well during the war," Lawrence said to George, referring to The French and Indian War that had recently concluded.

"Yes, we were more fortunate than most colonies. By the end of the war, the Cherokee had seceded much of their land in South Carolina to the British. Those acquisitions have allowed the colony to grow," George profoundly said. "And to our benefit, the British government had very little interference prior to the war," he added after taking a sip of his beer.

"Yes, it sounds as if South Carolina has been fortunate," Lawrence replied after inhaling a few puffs from his pipe.

"Although, since the cost of the war turned out to be so expensive, South Carolina is now feeling the effects of Britain's effort to pay off its war debt by taxing the colonies," George complained as he shifted in his chair to a more comfortable position.

"The situation in Virginia has been quite different. Britain's attempts to enact taxes are causing much unrest," Lawrence explained. "Have you heard that The Virginia House of Burgesses has passed the Virginia

Resolves in order to deny Parliament's right to tax the colonies in response to The Stamp Act?," Lawrence asked George. "The Stamp Act has affected nearly everything!," Lawrence complained as he placed his pipe on the table beside his chair. "A person can't even buy a newspaper or a deck of playing cards without paying a tax. It is easily understandable why it is causing so much anger since it affects legal documents and medicines as well," he added in frustration.

"I don't understand what King George thinks he is going to accomplish by causing such dissention," George retorted.

"And to add insult to injury, we should not be required to pay for the supplies of British troops stationed in each colony as The Quartering Act demands," Lawrence frowned as he thought about the tyrannical king.

"The colonies have made Britain a wealthy empire and we should be profiting as well from our contributions," George angrily exclaimed.

"I agree," Lawrence replied. "Many tobacco plantations are struggling to remain solvent since London merchants have precipitously reduced the price of tobacco. I believe that London's generous credit terms were just a ploy to drown tobacco growers in debt preventing them from paying back their loans," Lawrence continued to complain. "Fortunately, father diversified with other crops and livestock which has helped him sustain a profit," he continued as his anger gradually subsided.

"I can understand how this would cause unrest in Virginia," George responded.

"How is the rice crop doing this year?," Lawrence asked.

"Very well since the weather has been ideal this season," George confidently answered. "However, most South Carolina growers are upset with being taxed without representation," he continued.

"We definitely are being treated unfairly. Every day it seems to be more and more talk of breaking with Britain," Lawrence said.

"We are experiencing those same feelings in South Carolina," George said in agreement.

"Can't you two find something more pleasant to discuss?," Caroline interjected as she and Lavinia listened to their intense conversation.

"Pardon us ladies," Lawrence replied as he apologetically smiled at his wife and sister.

"I am so thankful the war is over," Lavinia said as she waved her fan in front of her face.

"So true, my dear, but all wars have lasting effects," George commented.

"Hopefully the good outweighs the bad," Lavinia optimistically responded.

"Yes, but unfortunately that's not always the case," Caroline replied. "Lawrence can attest to that," she added.

"What do you mean?," Lavinia asked.

"Lawrence was recently involved in a case related to the war. It had a rather sad outcome," Caroline answered while everyone looked at Lawrence with expressions of curiosity.

"Recently, I ruled over a trial involving treason and murder. There was a man who was trading secrets and selling weapons to the Algonquin Indians and the French. He was caught, tried and hung," Lawrence explained.

"Who did he murder?," Lavinia asked her brother.

"He stabbed and killed a British soldier when he was being apprehended," Lawrence answered.

"How could a man betray his own people and sell weapons to their enemy?," George wondered out loud.

"I don't understand why anyone would oppose our colonies and the freedom we aspire to," Caroline added.

"We do have to abide by the Crown's laws but fortunately we are displaced from them by distance," Lawrence commented.

"What a tragedy!," Lavinia exclaimed, trying to forget the image of a hanging man that her imagination had just conjured up.

"It has an even more tragic outcome. He has a young daughter who has to bear his shame," Lawrence said. "John Thompson, from the well-known Atherton family of Virginia, served as the prosecuting lawyer," he continued.

"I remember the Atherton name when I was in Virginia attending college," George recalled.

"John's father-in-law, General Robert Atherton, founded Atherton Village in the southeast area of the colony and has a successful tobacco plantation nearby," Lawrence reminded George.

"I remember General Atherton's plantation," George said as his face lit up.

"John has a wife, Rebecca, and a young teenage son, Benjamin, who is a few years older than Sarah," Lawrence elaborated. "Anyway, the facts were against the traitor and John knew that the unscrupulous and ambitious Alexander Drake, who served as his defense lawyer, couldn't convince the jury he was innocent," he continued.

"I have heard Drake does have quite an unscrupulous reputation," George recalled.

"Therefore, the convicted man's daughter will suffer also," Lawrence further explained.

"Oh, how dreadful!," Lavinia sadly declared.

"Yes, it is rather sad," Caroline added.

"Who was he?," Lavinia asked.

"Simon Bartram was his name," Lawrence answered.

"I wonder what motivated him to commit such an act?," George asked.

"In addition to his crimes, they say he was involved in numerous criminal activities in England and escaped to the colonies. Sadly, the colonies simply offered him more victims to gamble with and cheat. He looked at the gun sales to Indians as a way to expand his fortune," Lawrence explained. "Ironically, his act of treason caused the British government to confiscate all his assets and left him penniless," he continued.

"That is awful for his daughter. I wonder what will happen to her?," Lavinia asked.

"I heard her mother died when she was a young girl so she would have to be cared for by relatives. Although, Simon and his wife had none. Alexander looked after her until the authorities placed her with a foster family somewhere in Virginia. She'll remain with them until she becomes of age," Lawrence explained.

"Oh, that's awful!," Lavinia cried. "How old is she?," she asked.

"I heard she is around fifteen. Although, I am not quite sure since she never appeared in the courtroom." Lawrence informed. "I don't even recall ever hearing her name," he added.

"I thought we were supposed to be talking about something pleasant," Caroline reminded.

"Yes, dear. Thank you for reminding me," Lawrence teased his wife. "Again, I apologize to you ladies," he added.

"There is no need to apologize, dear brother!," Lavinia said. "I did find it rather interesting!," she said with a laugh while waving her fan.

"Are you all still planning to visit Virginia during Christmas?," Lawrence asked to shift the conversation.

"Yes! It will be nice to visit Penderley again," Lavinia said. "I am so looking forward to seeing mother and father!," she added with excitement. "I do wish we were closer, especially for Lucinda's sake," she continued while fondly watching the two young girls playing on the front lawn.

"Father is doing quite well. Although, mother is still dealing with her health issues," Lawrence explained. "But father is taking good care of her and we frequently visit Penderley to offer support. Although, they are fortunate to have Thomas and his family with them," he added.

"How are Martha and the boys?," Lavinia asked.

"Mother is in good hands with Martha taking care of her. Father and Thomas have taken Ethan and William under their wing and are grooming them to be the future caretakers of Penderley," Lawrence answered.

"We are so looking forward to being with all of them at Christmas!," Lavinia exclaimed. "It will be nice for Lucinda to see her cousins again," she added.

"Yes, it will be nice for the whole family to be together again!," Caroline interjected as Sarah and Lucinda came running towards the veranda from the front lawn.

"Are you enjoying the magnolias?," George asked Sarah.

"Yes, they smell heavenly!," Sarah exclaimed.

"Sarah, sometimes I wonder who you come to see...us or the magnolias!," George teased his niece while laughing over his words.

"She told me that when she grows up, she is going to have a bouquet of magnolias on her wedding day," Lucinda abruptly announced while Sarah blushed.

"Not only that, I am going to have them planted all around my house!," Sarah vehemently proclaimed while everyone smiled in amusement.

GARY ROWE

Charles City County, Virginia

Christmas, 1765

GARY ROWE

Chapter 3

The horses steadily trotted along the snow-covered wooded path while the anxious passengers in the coach looked forward to resting after their long journey to Penderley Plantation. The snow was slowly falling from the gloomy early winter sky as the last light of day was fading fast. As the evening approached, the light from the lanterns that were attached to the sides of the coach reflected off the snow-covered path to help guide them safely on their way. Once the coach made its way through the last part of the heavily wooded path, a brick Georgian mansion blanketed in snow suddenly appeared across the field ahead and the light shining from the windows created a picturesque scene as the beams reflected off the newly fallen snow.

A day earlier, Lavinia, George and Lucinda had arrived at Lawrence and Caroline's home in Williamsburg after their voyage northward from Magnolia Grove. The Lockwood family had planned on traveling to Penderley with Lawrence and his family after spending the night with them at Hemsworth House. Very early on the morning of their planned trip, the adults were abruptly awakened by shouts of joy after Sarah and Lucinda had gotten out of bed and peered out of Sarah's bedroom window. Their young eyes widened with excitement when they realized a light snowfall had dusted the town during the night. After considering the weather and the trip to Charles City County that lay ahead, the adults agreed it would be a good idea to get an early of a start as possible. During their daylong travel, as periods of heavy snowfall occurred, Sarah and Lucinda's excitement had grown while the adults had been constantly concerned with everyone's safety until their eventful journey came to an end.

As the horses came to a gradual stop at the front entrance of Penderley, the doorway underneath the white columned porch suddenly opened as a distinguished gray-haired gentleman stepped outside to greet his visitors. The driver of the coach quickly made his way to the ground to assist the passengers from the coach and tend to their trunks that had been safely secured at the rear.

"How is my beautiful daughter?," Nathaniel Eldridge asked with a big smile as Lavinia quickly exited the coach and climbed the brick steps to greet him. "And also my beautiful granddaughters!," he added as Sarah and Lucinda swiftly trailed behind Lavinia and rushed to his side.

"I am much better now that we have arrived safely!," Lavinia replied to her father as she fell into his open arms. "The roads are becoming quite treacherous! I am so glad the snow seems to be subsiding!," she added while Caroline hurried up the steps to join them.

"Hello, dear father!," Caroline said to her father-in-law as she gave Nathaniel a hug.

"It is so good to have all of you home!," Nathaniel said as he watched Lawrence and George supervising the servants while they transported the trunks to the porch.

"Thank you!," Lawrence said to the servants while he could be heard in the background by the others as he and George moved to the porch.

"Hello, sir," George said to his father-in-law as he reached outward to shake his hand.

"Father!," Lawrence warmly said while he bent forward to hug him. "We are looking forward to the family being all together during Christmas!," he joyfully added.

"I have missed you and mother so much!," Lavinia interjected. "How is mother?," she continued.

"She has had a spell with her gout these past few days," Nathaniel answered.

"I hope she is feeling better," Lavinia sympathetically replied.

"She is resting now but has been eagerly anticipating your arrival," Nathaniel answered to put his daughter at ease. "Please come in out of this unpleasant weather," he offered once everyone had gathered on the porch. "I'll have Josiah help your man tend to the trunks," Nathaniel continued as he glanced at Lawrence.

After everyone entered the capacious entrance hall, several house servants appeared to help everyone off with their coats while a distinguished heavy-set elderly woman appeared from the back part of the hall and was eagerly advancing toward the front door. She was elegantly dressed in a burgundy gown and her gray hair was neatly contained in a frilly white cap. Her right hand tightly held a walking cane as she cautiously moved forward with a slight limp.

"Grandma Abigail!," Sarah and Lucinda shouted almost in unison as they happily raced towards her.

"I thought I heard you all arriving!," Abigail said as Lavinia rushed into her arms.

"Mother! It is so nice to see you!," Lavinia said as she hugged and kissed her mother on the cheek as Sarah and Lucinda clung to their grandmother's side.

"I am so glad you all were able to come home for Christmas! I am so thrilled to have my entire family all together!," Abigail exclaimed.

"Yes, I can't wait to see my cousins!," Lucinda said as she echoed her grandmother's sentiments.

Before Lucinda could finish her words, Thomas and Martha along with their sons Ethan and William began to enter the entrance hall from the parlor.

"Do I hear our two bratty little cousins?," Ethan Eldridge teased as he ran up to scoop Lucinda in his arms while William did the same to Sarah.

"We aren't brats!," Lucinda said to Ethan while she began to laugh at her cousin's humor.

"What *are* you two little monsters then?," William teased as he looked at both girls with a big smile.

"You two are the monsters!," Sarah retorted as she started to giggle at the two amusing young men.

"You two behave!," Martha light-heartedly said to her two sons as they lowered both girls back to the floor. "We are so glad to have you all here!," she continued as she directed her attention to her in-laws.

"Brother! Sister! Happy Christmas!," Thomas joyfully said to Lawrence and Lavinia as he greeted them with open arms.

"You boys are growing up so fast!," Lavinia said as she focused her attention on Ethan and William while she reached to give both of them a hug. "I should say young men!," she continued while thinking it was difficult to believe her nephews were now approaching twenty years old.

"Uncle Lawrence and Uncle George!," Ethan said as he eagerly greeted the men while William followed suit.

"I know you all must be tired after your journey and would like to get settled," Nathaniel interjected as he walked to Abigail's side and looped his arm in hers. "Your trunks should be in your rooms shortly," he added as everyone began to gather at the foot of the stairs.

"You all know where your rooms are so make yourselves at home," Abigail said to her family in a welcoming voice as they began to climb the staircase.

"Once you all get situated, join us in the parlor," Thomas said as he and Martha began to enter the room to enjoy the warmth from the fireplace while Ethan, William, Nathaniel and Abigail followed behind.

"I'll have some refreshment waiting for you when you all return," Abigail said. "I'm sure you all are hungry after your long journey," she added as she glanced up the staircase while Nathaniel guided her through the doorway to the parlor.

Once they reached their rooms, Josiah soon arrived with the trunks allowing them to settle in for their lengthy stay. Sarah and Lucinda were elated when they learned they would be sharing a room located between each of their parents. Coincidentally, at the same time, Lawrence and George stepped out into the upstairs hallway to allow the ladies to take a few extra minutes to freshen up. Once the ladies joined the men in the upstairs hall chamber, Sarah and Lucinda excitedly led the way as they hurried to rejoin the family in the parlor.

"Just in time!," Abigail said as Sarah and Lucinda darted into the parlor while their parents followed them from behind. "Cook just brought cider and cakes for everyone to enjoy," she added while motioning to the sideboard against the wall. "Help yourselves!," Abigail continued as Sarah and Lucinda quickly dashed in that direction.

"Thank you mother," Lavinia said as she and George took heed to her mother's suggestion.

"They look delicious!," Caroline added as she admired the small gingerbread cakes arranged on a blue canton china platter while she and Lawrence stood beside Lavinia and George at the sideboard.

"Cook is famous for her gingerbread!," Abigail proudly said from the Chippendale sofa that she and Nathaniel shared near the fireplace.

"May I get you and father anything?," Lavinia said to her mother as she looked at her parents across the room.

"No thank you, dear," Abigail replied. "We all had a late supper," she continued while answering for everyone.

"Would you two ladies like a cup of hot cider?," Lawrence said to Sarah and Lucinda as he reached for the pitcher on the sideboard.

"Please!," the two girls said almost simultaneously as they anticipated tasting the spiced apple brew.

After the travelers had enjoyed their nourishment, they joined the rest of the family around the blazing fire burning in the fireplace. While the adults sat in the elegant but comfortable sofas and chairs that formed a seating group around the fireplace, Lucinda and Sarah sat on the fashionable Persian wool rug that anchored the room and began to engage in their own conversation as they enjoyed the warmth of the glowing fire.

"It is wonderful to have all of us together!," Nathaniel joyfully said while everyone claimed a seat. "You know your mother and I are not getting any younger!," he teased.

"Speak for yourself!," Abigail said to return his playfulness. "I may be getting older but I am not giving up on life!," she continued as she thought about her burdensome health issues.

"Don't talk like that!," Martha said. "We couldn't imagine our lives without you two!," she fondly added.

"So true, my dear!," Thomas concurred with his wife. "If we didn't have you two, who would help us keep our sanity during these unsettled times?," Thomas teased as he ironically thought about the current political situation in the colony.

"We are certainly living in troubled times," Nathaniel agreed.

"Uncle Lawrence, how is the mood in Williamsburg?," Ethan asked his uncle as he joined the conversation.

"There definitely are times of unrest. The Stamp Act recently provoked another act of protest. At the end of October, George Mercer, who recently arrived from England as the appointed stamp distributer for Virginia, was accosted by a concourse of gentlemen on the east end of Duke of Gloucester Street," Lawrence explained.

"What happened?," William asked as the conversation began to draw his interest.

"He was on his way to meet the governor in the capitol and a group of men demanded to know whether he intended to act as a commissioner under the Stamp Act. He attempted to pacify the crowd but they threatened him with violence and the next day he resigned," Lawrence informed.

"That sounds so dangerous!," Lavinia said as she thought about the violence that an angry crowd could ignite. "That could be unsafe for innocent bystanders," she added.

"There is never a dull moment in the capital," Caroline said as she added to the conversation.

"Speaking of excitement in the capital, tell us about the infamous trial of Simon Bartram," Thomas prompted. "I found it to be very interesting when I read about it in *The Virginia Gazette* earlier this year," Thomas recalled.

"The trial did get a lot of publicity. There is no other way to describe him but as being a traitor. He was selling weapons and secrets to the French and Indians during the war. And when he was being apprehended he stabbed a British officer killing him," Lawrence explained.

"I don't know how Alexander Drake could have been so confident to think that he could convince the jury to find that traitor innocent," Thomas reasoned.

"That is what I thought when we discussed it this past summer," George recalled.

"John Thompson presented his case and all the evidence precisely and accurately. Alexander was furious when he lost. He has always been so ambitious and would slight anyone to achieve what he wants. I think most of his anger stemmed from being overlooked for judgeship since he had such high hopes of being appointed," Lawrence said. "I believe he is rather bitter about it," he added.

"Lawrence, be sure to give John my regards when you see him. And tell him to be sure to pass them on to Rebecca and General Atherton," Nathaniel interjected.

"I certainly will, father," Lawrence assured.

"I don't feel sorry for Alexander in the least. I keep thinking about Simon's poor daughter who has to live with her father's shame," Caroline said as she kept to the subject at hand.

"Well, hopefully she's strong enough to overcome this and start a new life for herself," Lawrence replied.

"I just hope she is getting the proper guidance and support she needs while still being an impressionable young girl," Lavinia added.

"I hope so for her sake," Martha responded. "I'm sure that is hard to digest when your own father is accused of being a traitor," she added.

"Well, you all will never have that to worry about," Abigail said to her children as she interjected the conversation. "I am thankful your father has been such an honest and upstanding role model to you all," she continued while she fondly gazed at her husband.

"And you have been a wonderful blessing to me!," Nathaniel said as he returned his wife's affection.

"Yes, we are very fortunate to have such wonderful parents," Lavinia lovingly said to her mother and father.

"I always remember how father would tell us that honesty, dedication and hard work will lead to success," Thomas remembered. "It gives one self-worth," he continued.

"Oh yes, I remember that well," Lawrence said. "And all that hard work has definitely paid off. It looks as if the plantation is doing well," Lawrence said to his father and brother.

"We are faring pretty well," Nathaniel replied.

"Father was wise when he diversified with other crops. The simple fact that we did not have to seek an excessive amount of loans from London creditors has saved us from a lot of financial hardship," Thomas said. "We have been able to make a decent profit," he added.

"Ethan and William have been learning fast and we continue to make strides," Nathaniel confirmed. "We must keep Penderley going strong so it can be passed down to the next generation," he continued.

"Don't' worry grandfather, we will make you proud," Ethan said with conviction.

"We will be nothing but successful!," William added.

"Our family has been blessed and we must be thankful to God for what he has given us," Nathaniel humbly acknowledged.

"Yes, and we have lots of festivities planned to celebrate the days leading up to Christmas!," Abigail happily said to her family. "I'm getting tired just thinking about our busy schedule!," she added.

"With that being said, I think it is time for your mother and I to retire for the evening," Nathaniel said while he stood to help Abigail arise from the sofa.

"I know Sarah and Lucinda must be tired after their long day," Abigail said as she looked at her granddaughters deep in conversation while sitting on the floor close to the fire. "You two ladies need your rest so you can enjoy your day tomorrow!," Abigail continued as she noticed Sarah beginning to yawn. "Your grandfather and I will tuck you in!," she suggested as they slowly arose from the floor.

"We will be right behind you. I am becoming rather tired myself," Lavinia said to her parents. "Sleep well ladies! I'll check on you both before your father and I go to bed," she said to her daughter and niece while she stood to hug and kiss her parents.

"Sleep well, dear. Your father and I will be up shortly," Caroline said to Sarah.

"I think I will be leaving you all for the evening as well," Ethan said thinking about the chores that would be awaiting him and William early in the morning.

"You two monsters sleep well!," William teased his two young cousins as he arose from his chair to leave the room with Ethan.

"You are the monster!," Sarah retorted with a giggle as they all began to leave the room.

"Good night everyone," Lawrence said as the three remaining couples shifted seats to get closer to the fireplace.

"We probably should think about retiring as well," Martha said to Thomas as she sat next to him on the sofa.

"I still have some last-minute preparations to make for our travel," she continued.

"Martha and I had previously planned a trip to visit her aunt in Petersburg for a couple of days. We will be leaving the day after tomorrow," Thomas explained when he noticed the look of curiosity on everyone's face. "How would you and Caroline, along with George and Lavinia, like to join us," Thomas suggested as he looked at each couple.

"We appreciate the offer, but I think George and I will remain at Penderley because I would like to spend as much time with mother and father as possible. But if Lawrence and Caroline would like to go, George and I will be glad to look after Sarah," Lavinia offered as she glanced at Lawrence and Caroline. "I know she and Lucinda would enjoy their time together as well," she continued.

"I will enjoy the time with Nathaniel and the boys discussing our crops. I will have to listen to them tell me how much better their tobacco is than my rice," George said with humor while all three men laughed.

"That does sound like something they would say," Thomas said as he continued to smile.

"We would love to join you," Caroline said as she saw the look of approval on Lawrence's face. "It would be nice to see your Aunt Verity again," she added.

"We can take the opportunity to do a little Christmas shopping in town before we return," Martha suggested to Caroline. "A friend of mine owns a millinery shop and she has the finest things! And I know how much you love hats!," Martha joyfully continued.

"That would be lovely!," Caroline replied.

"Hopefully the weather will have improved by the time we leave," Thomas optimistically said.

"I'll second that motion," Lawrence responded.

"Even though it is going to be a busy time, I am looking forward to all the activities we have planned during Christmas and spending it with you all!," Martha exclaimed.

"And so are we!," Caroline excitedly agreed.

As they continued to discuss the upcoming events and festivities, the remaining embers of the fading fire signaled the conclusion that it was time to retire for the night. While the three couples arose from their seats and casually walked toward the entrance hall to climb the stairs, their silent thoughts relished in the joy of the Christmas season and also with hopes that God would continue to bless each of their families in the coming year.

Chapter 4

The following morning when Martha opened the wooden shutters to her and Thomas's bedroom, a brilliant sun had begun to rise in the clear blue sky over Penderley. During the night, the snow had gradually ceased and the sky had cleared setting the stage for a brighter day ahead. The temperatures hurriedly rose as the morning progressed and the warmth of the sun caused the snow to quickly begin to melt.

"If this keeps up, by the end of the day it won't be much snow left on the ground," Thomas predicted.

"That is fine with me. Snow is beautiful when it is falling but it does become a nuisance when one has to travel," Martha replied. "That will make our trip much more pleasant when we set out early tomorrow morning," she continued.

Early the next day, Thomas and Martha – along with Lawrence and Caroline – set out on their journey not long after the sun began to rise. Thomas's weather prediction came true and the trip proved to be bearable as Josiah safely steered the horses from the driver seat of the coach along the damp roads caused by the melting snow. By late afternoon, as the horses pulled the coach into the town of Petersburg, Martha was eager to see her aunt that she had grown to love so dearly. As Josiah drove the horses at a steady gait through the center of town, memories of Martha's childhood came rushing back like a wave from the ocean as it rushed to the seashore.

Her aunt and uncle, Charles and Verity Attwood, had taken Martha in and raised her as their own after the untimely and tragic death of her parents when she was a young girl of five. Martha's parents were returning from Richmond after visiting friends when the weather took a drastic turn for the worse. The torrential rains along with the loud claps of thunder and the fierce bolts of lightning created a harrowing journey. When the driver attempted to control the horses, the coach slipped off the muddy road and into a ravine killing both her parents and the driver of the coach. After the unfortunate incident, it was determined that poor visibility from the weather had contributed to the cause of the tragic accident.

As she remembered the devastating event, her feelings of pain slowly faded away when the coach passed the building that was formerly her uncle's general store. A smile gradually appeared across her face and her heart warmed as she recalled the first time she saw Thomas Eldridge. Martha fondly remembered how her heart fluttered when their eyes met as the handsome man entered the store. Later, Thomas admitted that what he thought would be an uneventful trip to Petersburg to purchase supplies for the plantation actually changed his life in an astonishing way.

After Thomas and Martha married, Martha regularly returned to Petersburg to visit the couple that she viewed in her heart and had come to love so dearly as her true parents. Over the years, Charles and Verity occasionally traveled to Penderley to visit their niece and her new family. After Charles's unexpected death, two years earlier, Martha offered her aunt a home with her and Thomas. However, Verity felt she belonged in Petersburg and wanted to remain close to her friends and the familiar place where she had built a life with Charles.

When the horses pulled the coach onto River Street and along the curb in front of Aunty Verity's house, the sound of the horses and the rattling of the halting coach brought Martha's wondering thoughts back to the present. While Martha hurriedly stepped out of the coach and quickly climbed the steps to the porch, the front door suddenly flung open as Verity gracefully dashed to greet her.

"Aunt Verity!," Martha exclaimed as she raced into her aunt's open arms.

"I've missed you so much, dear!," Verity happily said to Martha as they lingered in each other's embrace.

"And I've missed you more!," Martha lovingly replied to her aunt.

"Welcome everyone!," Verity said as the others exited the coach and gathered at the foot of the steps. "Please come into the house out of the cold! I have a warm fire burning in the fireplace and coffee and spice cake for everyone to enjoy. I know you all must be weary after your journey," she continued as the rest of her niece's family joined them on the porch.

"That would be so nice!," Caroline replied. "It was a rather cold and damp journey," she continued.

"It has been a while since Caroline and I have seen you but it is always a pleasure," Lawrence politely said to Verity. "Thank you for having us," he continued.

"The pleasure is all mine," Verity kindly replied as she turned to look down at Josiah standing near the coach. "Hello, Josiah. Thank you for bringing my niece and her family to me safe and sound," Verity called to the driver from the porch. "If you would pull the coach around, I'll have Sam meet you out back," she continued, referring to her servant and handyman.

"Thank you, Miss Verity," Josiah replied as he turned to accomplish his duty.

When everyone had entered the entrance hallway, a seasonal fragrance of fresh pine lingered throughout the house from the fresh greenery, pinecones and holly berries that had been used to decorate the banister rail and fireplace mantles in the house.

"Oh, how lovely!," Martha exclaimed as memories from her childhood entered her mind.

"When you were a child, I remember how you used to love to decorate for Christmas!," Verity fondly said to her niece as she ushered everyone into the front parlor. "Please make yourselves at home. Sam found some nice boxwood and pine in the woods on the outskirts of town and we decorated just for you!," Verity proudly exclaimed as everyone sat down on the comfortable furniture arranged near the fireplace.

"Everything looks so festive!," Caroline said as she assessed the cheerfully decorated room.

"I normally don't decorate for Christmas, but I knew you were coming!," Verity said as an expression of delight appeared on her face. "It can be lonesome sometimes since Charles is no longer with us. Especially during this time of year," she continued with a tone of melancholy in her voice.

"As I've offered many times, you do know that you have an open invitation to come and live with us at Penderley," Martha reminded her aunt as she glanced at Thomas.

"Yes, we would love to have you near us," Thomas assured Verity while being prompted by the expression on his wife's face.

"You are both so dear to me. It may come to that in a few years, but for now I'd like to stay in my own home and near my close friends," Aunt Verity replied. "And I have so many memories of your Uncle Charles here," she continued as she arose from her chair to pour everyone a cup of coffee from the tea table in the center of the seating group.

"I understand, Aunt Verity," Martha responded as she arose to assist her aunt with serving while noticing by her aunt's facial expression that Verity was fondly remembering the past.

"The town seems to change every time we come to visit," Thomas said to Verity as she handed him a cup of coffee.

"Since the town expanded up the hill three years ago, it has added about twenty-eight acres so we are definitely growing." Verity explained as she sat back down in her chair.

"Caroline and I do want to do a little shopping while we are here," Martha noted. "I hear there are a few new shops in town," she added while she finished serving everyone coffee and cake.

"Yes, there are a few places you will definitely like. Jane Hamilton always asks me about you every time I visit her shop," Verity replied to Martha.

"How is Jane? I hope my mail order that I placed a few weeks ago has arrived," Martha wondered out loud as she returned to her seat beside Thomas on the sofa.

"Jane seems troubled these days. She and her husband have recently taken a young girl into their home who recently lost her father. The girl had no other relatives. They were so kind to take her in but she seems quite unappreciative and is quite a handful," Verity explained.

"How ungrateful. She should be thankful someone cared enough to come to her aid," Caroline added to the conversation.

"One would think so, wouldn't they?," Lawrence added. "Hopefully she'll come to realize how fortunate she is to be taken in and cared for," he continued.

"I agree. I don't quite understand the situation. It's a mystery why that young girl is so angry," Verity responded with a look of wonder on her face. "Well enough about that!," she continued. "I want to focus on enjoying our time together!"

"Yes! I want to savor every moment with my dear aunt!," Martha affectionately added.

"Let me show you to your rooms and I'll let you all get settled so you can recuperate from your journey," Verity offered. "Again, I am so looking forward to our time together!," she continued while everyone arose from their seats. "I have a nice meal planned for us later this evening!," she added.

Later that evening, while everyone enjoyed the delicious meal and joyful conversation as they lingered around the dining room table, Verity shared fond memories of Martha's childhood. Verity explained with much sentiment how Martha had brought her and Charles so much joy and happiness when they had taken her in after the tragic and unexpected death of her parents. Verity also described, with much animation, the happiness she felt when Martha had told her she had fallen in love with the handsome Thomas Eldridge. Martha lovingly expressed how fortunate she was to have the love and support of Verity and Charles and how they had such a positive effect on her life. As Martha thought about her fortunate circumstances, her mind suddenly wandered to the young girl that Jane Hamilton and her husband had taken into their home. Martha hoped the young girl would realize her good fortune and be grateful and appreciative for the love and support the Hamilton's had to offer in her time of need.

"Well, I know you all must be exhausted after a long day!," Verity realized. "And we do have a full day ahead of us tomorrow!," she reminded everyone as they arose from the table to retire for the evening.

The next morning, Martha and Caroline decided to visit the new shops in town before joining Verity and a few close friends for a holiday celebration later that afternoon. As Thomas and Lawrence escorted the ladies into town, the mid-morning sun peaked through occasional passing clouds while adding warmth to the chilly late December day. Verity stayed behind to make the final preparations for their social gathering. After spending the morning exploring the new shops and being delighted with their purchases, they made a final stop at Jane Hamilton's to pick up Martha's order before returning to Aunt Verity's house.

As Martha and Caroline entered the millinery shop, Jane was busy unpacking merchandise and tidying shelves that had been disheveled by earlier shoppers. A teenage girl was standing behind the counter and immediately looked up at the ladies entering the shop when she heard the jingling of the bell that was attached to the doorknob. The teenage girl glared at the two ladies in their elegant finery as they gracefully entered the shop. Their beautiful wool cloaks, stylish hats, and fur-lined muffs immediately caught her attention. As the girl glanced at herself in a nearby looking glass, she immediately recognized the stark contrast. Their aristocratic appearance reminded the young girl of the elegant clothes she once wore and the finer things she previously possessed that were no longer hers.

"Good day, Jane," Martha said to greet the shopkeeper as she turned to see who was entering her establishment.

"Martha, it's so nice to see you! Your order arrived yesterday," Jane replied to her customer and friend.

"I'm so glad. I was afraid it wouldn't arrive before Christmas," Martha responded. "This is my sister-in-law, Caroline, who is visiting from Williamsburg. She and her husband, Judge Eldridge, are joining us at Penderley for Christmas," Martha informed Jane as the two ladies smiled at each other and nodded their heads. "We are so glad the family will all be together!," Martha added.

When the young girl heard Martha introduce her sister-in-law, her head jerked upward and her eyes opened wider while she began to listen more attentively to their conversation.

"It is very nice to meet you, Mrs. Eldridge," Jane said to Caroline.

"Please, call me Caroline. Your shop is lovely!," Caroline responded as she turned her head to glance around the room and noticed the fine hats and colorful accessories that adorned the shelves.

"Well, thank you!," she replied with an appreciative smile.

"Her shop does have a wonderful reputation!," Martha complimented while an expression of pride appeared on Jane's face.

"I have your order all packed and ready to go," Jane said to Martha.

"Dear, would you please get Mrs. Eldridge's order from the backroom," Jane said to the dark brown-haired girl as she glared at the two ladies with a heavy frown on her face while she stomped out of the room.

"Please accept my apologies for her rudeness. She recently lost her father and Mr. Hamilton and I have taken her in since she has no other relatives. She can be difficult at times but we are trying to be patient with her," Jane explained as she walked behind the counter.

"Oh, what a lovely hat!," Caroline said as she noticed a bonnet on the shelf behind the counter that caught her attention.

"My sister-in-law loves hats!," Martha said to explain Caroline's excitement.

"I must try it on!," Caroline said as Jane reached for the hat on the shelf to hand it to her potential customer.

While Caroline was admiring herself in the looking glass that rested on the counter, the girl returned from the backroom carrying the packages she was sent to retrieve. While being self-absorbed in her own thoughts, the young girl clumsily tripped over her feet and fell quickly forward but caught herself on the edge of the counter before falling to the floor.

"Please! Be careful with the merchandise!," Jane snapped at the girl, while the girl struggled to contain her anger.

Once the girl had regained her composure, she continued to stew in her anger and resentment as she glared at the two ladies. As she looked upward past Martha and Caroline and out of the picture window that faced the street, she noticed two men standing beside the waiting coach. Once she recognized one of the men, who in her mind, brought about the demise of her father and reduced her to her current station in life, her anger began to rage like a violent storm. The name Lawrence Eldridge would remain embedded in her memory for the rest of her life. In her mind, she justified her father's innocence and blamed the judge and prosecuting lawyer for his death. Her father's defense lawyer, Alexander Drake, had pointed out the two men while she sat in the coach outside the courthouse. By the tone in Alexander's voice and his angry words of defeat, she sensed that he too felt hostility and disdain for those two men. From that moment, she swore to herself that Lawrence Eldridge and John Thompson would pay dearly for what they had done to her and her father.

The girl's father, Simon Bartram, had been born into poverty in the worst part of London. Dolly, Simon's mother, had been abandoned at an early age. As she grew into her teenaged years, she took to prostitution in order to survive. During one of her drunken stupors, Simon became the product of one of her many trysts. Being brought up in the midst of this undesirable lifestyle, Simon learned about deceit and trickery from an early age. Dolly soon found there was a benefit to hovering near gambling houses as it allowed her the chance to help a fortunate gambler celebrate after having a lucky night at the tables. Dolly occasionally had repeat customers and a few of her inamoratos would teach Simon about gambling and playing cards for money. Simon soon perfected his ability to cheat and win at cards and, unknowing at the time, it allowed him to perfect a dishonest craft that would temporarily benefit him later in life.

When his mother died while he was a young teenager, after her unsavory lifestyle took its toll on her health, Simon was left to fend for himself on the rough streets of London. Due to his mature looks, he soon learned he could easily pass for a much older man and began to frequent gambling houses with hopes of attaining financial gain. Simon developed a taste for gin since it was cheap, easily assessible and sold everywhere since no license was required to sell it. After developing the ability to easily hold his liquor due to his excessive drinking, he would pretend to be drunk during card games to make his opponents think he had lost control of his senses.

During one of his card games, Simon met a woman named Opal equal in nature to his conniving ways. Simon and Opal soon became lovers and over time became more and more desperate to make money. Together, they learned it was best to use aliases to evade authorities and ease their fears of being recognized in the gambling circuit.

One night, while lying in bed after a passionate encounter, they came up with a scheme to further advance their desire for money. Opal would enter into gambling games, separate from Simon, while they would pretend they had no association with one another. Simon would work one side of the room and pretend to be drunk while playing cards. Opal, working the other side of the room, would lure drunken winners with the pretense of a night of passion only to con them out of their cash and other belongings. Opal also found the benefit of occasionally waiting outside of raffling shops and luring well-dressed gentlemen into offering to place money on a raffle for her. When the unsuspecting victim would present her with the prize, Opal would tease him until he was drunk and when he passed out she would proceed to steal all of his personal items.

During one unfortunate incident, Simon surprisingly lost a card game to a man who displayed a little more expertise at playing cards than himself. After his defeat, Simon motioned to Opal to try and lure the man into her web. However, not knowing to them, the officer had previously observed the two of them and caught-on to their scheme. As Simon and Opal attempted to escape down the alley behind the gambling house, the officer pulled out his gun and started firing at the fleeing pair. As the bullets from the officer's gun flew through the air, a lone pellet struck Opal in the back and she immediately fell to the ground. Simon, severely shaken and panic-stricken, continued to run and escaped the misfortune that had befallen him. He soon learned of Opal's fate as the news of the tragic event spread through the gambling circuit.

For fear of being constantly searched for by the authorities, Simon decided it best to leave London behind. After a short deliberation, and often hearing tales of the opportunities on the other side of the Atlantic Ocean during card games, he decided to jump on the next ship to the American colonies. His ship first landed in Alexandria, in the northern part of the Virginia Colony. Simon's initial intention was to continue on northward to Philadelphia or New York thinking that a more populated area would provide him with a good number of victims to continue his career of thievery and deceit. However, he deducted that it would be a better idea to lay low in a more rural area, at least for the time being, with hopes of evading the traveling news of his escape from London.

As soon as Simon settled in the Virginia Colony, it didn't take him long to find the best places to gamble in the surrounding areas. During a gambling game in a warehouse on the Alexandria waterfront, he met a seductive woman by the name of Daisy. Her dark brown hair and voluptuous figure reminded him of Opal. When the two shared a look of mutual attraction, they quickly became lovers and started a life of gambling and cheating similar to the tactics that he and Opal had perfected.

When Daisy unexpectedly learned she was with child, Simon's initial reaction was of anger and outrage. However, after becoming used to the idea of being a father, he gradually accepted the fact and realized he had come to terms with the situation. As their daughter grew, Simon and Daisy taught her the craft of shoplifting to help with their survival. The young girl soon showed signs of drawing pleasure from the benefits of her dishonesty and developed a love of money and a taste for the finer things in life.

At one eventful card game, during the final years of conflict between the American colonies and the French and Indians, Simon luckily won big. As he wallowed in his good fortune, he had no idea this good luck would eventually lead to his downfall. Through connections, he learned how he could use his winnings to make even more money. He soon was involved in buying illegally obtained weapons and began selling them to the enemy for a high profit. His newfound wealth allowed him to lavish Daisy and his daughter with expensive gifts and the best things that money could buy. This only added to his daughter's lust of money and her conscience never allowed her to believe there was anything wrong with the way they had acquired such things. After Simon achieved what he viewed as success, Daisy sadly died when their daughter was ten years old. Simon's continued wealth allowed his daughter to move in better circles and to associate with better classes while she and her father kept his true dealings a secret.

Even though his daughter knew about his dishonest dealings, Simon attempted to keep her knowledge at a minimum while he continued to shower her with clothes and trinkets to win her affection. He spoiled her excessively which in turn made her a very selfish and self-centered girl. When Simon was eventually caught and convicted of his crimes, he was stripped of his assets by the British government and his teenage daughter had lost both her parents and was left penniless with no means of support.

While the bitter girl was remembering the material possessions that her father had lavished upon her along with what she had lost due to his conviction, Caroline's excited voice forced her wandering mind back to the present.

"I love the hat! I'll take it!," Caroline excitedly said to Jane as she removed the hat from her head.

"Wonderful!," Jane replied as she reached downward to retrieve a hatbox from underneath the counter.

While Martha and Caroline concluded their business and exchanged wishes of Happy Christmas to Jane, it was difficult not to notice the impolite girl as she stood behind the counter and continued to display her unpleasant demeanor. Martha wondered what her friend was thinking when she and her husband decided to take in such an obviously disturbed and angry young girl.

As Martha and Caroline left the shop with their purchases and the jingling of the bell on the closing door had silenced, the vengeful girl vowed to herself that those two men had not heard the last from her. John Thompson and Lawrence Eldridge would regret the day they heard the name Simon Bartram.

Atherton County, Virginia

Christmas, 1771

GARY ROWE

Chapter 5

"Good morning, mother," Benjamin Thompson cheerfully said as he entered the dining room while Horace, his white Spitz, happily walked beside him wagging his tail.

"Did you sleep well, dear?," Rebecca asked as Benjamin bent forward to kiss her on the cheek while she sat in a chair at the table.

"Very well, thank you. It is so good to be home!," Benjamin answered as the inviting smell of coffee led him to the sideboard to pour himself a cup.

"I can see Horace is delighted you have returned!," Rebecca said as she glanced at the happy canine while Horace found a comfortable spot on the floor and continued to keep his eyes on Benjamin.

"I can't believe how much he has grown!," Benjamin replied. "He was just a puppy when I left. I'm surprised he remembers me!," Benjamin continued as he fondly looked at his faithful companion resting on the floor.

"Cook made pancakes just for you!," Rebecca said as she smiled at her son.

"That is one of the things I missed most while away, especially the maple syrup!," Benjamin replied with a smile as he piled a few cakes on his plate. "I remember, even as a little boy, how grandfather would plunge each piece of his pancake under the syrup and sopping it good before he ate it," he happily recalled while generously pouring syrup on his pancakes.

"Yes, and he is still doing that!," Rebecca laughingly declared.

"And that's another reason I am so happy to be home!," Benjamin jokingly said as he placed his plate on the table and sat down in the Chippendale side chair next to her.

"I know I have told you a million times but your father and I, along with your grandfather, are so glad to have you back with us!," Rebecca happily responded.

For a few moments, Rebecca vividly recalled in her mind the day her husband John told her their son was coming home. To her, Benjamin's two-year absence seemed like an eternity and the announcement that he was returning to America was a welcome one. Rebecca's father, General Robert Atherton, thought it best that her son be educated in England at the school he so fondly remembered as a young man. Robert strongly felt that a superior education at Cambridge would not only make Benjamin a more well-rounded man but more importantly would provide him with the knowledge to manage a successful and profitable plantation. While Rebecca sat quietly thinking about her son's two-year absence, she realized that he had changed during his time abroad. Benjamin had become more responsible and his classic facial features, thick light-brown hair, and slim athletic build had matured to create a strikingly handsome man.

"Where is father and grandfather this morning?," Benjamin asked as he interrupted her thoughts.

"They got an early start this morning and decided to ride out into the fields to check on plantation business," Rebecca explained.

"Why did they not wait for me?," Benjamin replied. "I have a lot to catch up on!," he continued.

"They decided to let you rest and take a little time to get used to being back home. Don't worry, dear." Rebecca responded as she saw the look of disappointment on his face. "They will be putting you to work soon enough!," she continued while resting her hand on his forearm to give it a light squeeze.

"I am ready now!," Benjamin enthusiastically responded.

"Remember, your father and I will be leaving for Williamsburg the day after next. We are so looking forward to the Governor's Christmas Ball," Rebecca informed. "Are you sure you won't change your mind and join us?," she asked as she raised her cup to take a sip of warm coffee.

"Thank you, mother. But I think I'll stay here and spend time with grandfather. Although, be sure to give Judge and Mrs. Eldridge my regards," Benjamin said. "It seems like yesterday when father would take me with him to Williamsburg on business and the first time he introduced me to the Eldridges," Benjamin continued as he began to recall the generational ties between his family and the Eldridge family.

Benjamin remembered that Judge Eldridge's grandfather, Jeremiah Eldridge, had been under the command of Benjamin's grandfather – the well-respected General Robert Atherton – during his service in the

British Army. Due to his service, Jeremiah's son Nathaniel had been acquainted with General Atherton since they were both young men and was well aware of his reputation as being one of the youngest generals and his heroic accomplishments for the British Crown.

King George had rewarded General Atherton with a land grant in the southern part of the Virginia Colony a year earlier than his grant to Nathaniel. However, General Atherton did not sail to America to settle his land until two years after Nathaniel had already left for America. The general's commitment to his military service in England had delayed his arrival in the colonies but Nathaniel and General Atherton would eventually become neighbors after he sailed to America to claim his land.

Once arriving in the southern part of the Virginia Colony, General Atherton built a plantation house befitting to his status and began to grow tobacco. While establishing himself in the colony and being introduced to Virginia's gentry, he soon met Elizabeth Ludwell of neighboring Surry County. After the couple married, Elizabeth gave birth to a daughter, Rebecca. After sharing nearly ten years of happiness, Robert was heartbroken when his beloved wife Elizabeth passed away when Rebecca was eight years old. Rebecca grew into a beautiful young lady and on one particular occasion, while visiting Williamsburg with her father, she was introduced to a young lawyer by the name of John Thompson. Not long after Rebecca and John were married, she gave birth to a son who they named Benjamin. Within a year after the birth of his grandson, General Atherton took approximately 60 acres from his extensive plantation and laid out the little river town called Atherton Village in 1752.

"I hear their daughter, Sarah, is growing into a lovely young lady. Are you sure you won't change your mind?,"

Rebecca teasingly asked Benjamin. "I don't believe you two have seen each other since you were both young children," she added while her words brought Benjamin's thoughts back to the present.

"Grandfather and I have plantation business to discuss. I can manage that part of my life myself," Benjamin teased. "Have you forgotten that I am a grown man now?," he added with a laugh.

"You do know that I want nothing but the best for you, dear," Rebecca affectionately replied.

"You know that grandfather will be passing the reigns to me one day," Benjamin proudly said. "However, hopefully no time soon," he continued on a more serious note.

"Don't worry, dear. I don't think your grandfather will be leaving us any time soon!," she said to dismiss her son's absurd thought as her husband and father suddenly appeared in the doorway.

"Father! Grandfather!," Benjamin said as he quickly arose from his seat while Horace raised his head off the floor and wagged his tail as the two men entered the room.

"Ahh, the two other most important men in my life have returned!," Rebecca affectionately said as John bent to give his wife a kiss on the cheek before taking the seat on the other side of her.

"Did I hear my name?," General Atherton playfully said to his daughter as he took his seat at the head of the mahogany pedestal table.

"Benjamin was just saying how eager he is to start helping you with the plantation," Rebecca informed.

"I am looking forward to that also. We are doing quite well. I just paid off our loans to London creditors and we are successfully turning a good profit," Robert proudly said.

"That's good news, grandfather," Benjamin replied as his grandfather eyed his pancakes.

"John, I worked up an appetite while we were out. Don't you think it's time we had another round of pancakes?," Robert asked his son-in-law.

"There are still plenty in the chafing dish on the sideboard!," Rebecca declared as she winked at Benjamin while recalling their earlier conversation.

"I'll leave you to enjoy," Benjamin said as he arose from his seat. "I thought I would check with the servants to see if the coach and horses' harnesses have been prepared for your journey," he thoughtfully added.

"That was one of the next things on my to-do list," John informed. "Thank you, Benjamin," he added while proudly realizing his son was becoming a responsible young man.

"That's nice of you, dear. That reminds me, when we return from Williamsburg, I was hoping we could gather some boxwood and magnolia leaves to decorate the house for Christmas," Rebecca suggested.

"That will be a good job for Benjamin and me whenever you give us the word," Robert happily said to his daughter.

"It will be nice to decorate together as a family! It's been a long time since we were all together during Christmas," Rebecca said with sentiment as Benjamin disappeared through the doorway while Horace happily walked by his side.

Chapter 6

On the day of their departure from Atherton County, Rebecca and John set out shortly after sunrise on a bright and clear but briskly cold late December day. After staying the night at an inn at the usual half-way point in Surry County, they awoke refreshed from their previous day's journey and arrived in Williamsburg by late-afternoon. As the driver of the coach guided the horses beside the brick walkway in front of Hemsworth House, Caroline was keeping watch at one of the front parlor windows while she and Lawrence anticipated their arrival.

"Rebecca and John have arrived!," Caroline excitedly said to Lawrence while he relaxed in a chair by the warm fire burning in the fireplace.

Caroline quickly walked from the parlor to the entrance hall as Lawrence followed behind her. As she eagerly opened the front door, Rebecca and John stepped out of the coach and quickly made their way to the opening door in anticipation of the warm fire they knew would be waiting for them.

"Come in out of the cold!," Caroline invitingly said as Lawrence appeared in the doorway behind her. "We are so glad you accepted our invitation," she continued.

"Thank you for having us!," Rebecca said as she and John climbed the brick steps to greet them.

"Please come in," Lawrence said in a welcoming tone. "We have a warm fire waiting," Lawrence continued as he shook John's hand while they stepped into the entrance hall.

"I thought you may like to rest by the fire while your coach is taken to the stables around back and then we'll have your trunk delivered to your room," Caroline suggested while she and Lawrence helped John and Rebecca with removing their coats.

"I would welcome the chance to get warm! The journey was rather a cold one," Rebecca replied while they entered the front parlor.

"Would you all care for a glass of brandy?," Lawrence offered as he turned to a bureau with a crystal decanter and glasses resting on a silver tray.

"Yes, that will definitely help us get warm," John said as he glanced at Rebecca and saw a look of affirmation on her face.

"We are so looking forward to the ball tomorrow evening!," Rebecca said as she and Caroline sat down on the sofa facing the fireplace.

"Our new governor is quite different than Governor Botetourt," Caroline replied. "It is rumored that Lord Dunmore was reluctant to accept the position in Virginia and wanted to remain as Governor of New York,"

Caroline continued while Lawrence handed her and Rebecca a glass of brandy.

"I hear that Lord Dunmore's wife Charlotte and their six children are still living in Scotland," Rebecca said as she took a sip from her glass while Lawrence and John sat down in wing chairs that flanked each side of the sofa.

"Yes, he felt our warmer climate was unhealthy and prevented his family from relocating with him," Caroline said as she recalled the rumor of his ridiculous assumption.

"Well, hopefully he will overcome that misconception and his family will join him soon," Rebecca responded while quietly wondering why the new governor would feel that way.

"Maybe we will get a better impression of him when we see how well he hosts his ball," Caroline said with a laugh while Lawrence and John amusingly listened to their wives gossiping.

"I hear is it going to be a grand affair!," Rebecca replied.

"I am sure we will see quite a few people we know," Caroline said.

"Where is your lovely daughter, Sarah? I thought we might have the pleasure of seeing her," Rebecca said to Caroline. "She must be a beautiful young lady now," she continued.

"Yes! It's hard to believe she turned sixteen a few months ago," Caroline replied. "She is with Lawrence's family at Penderley. Her grandmother is failing in health and she is helping Lawrence's family care for her," Caroline explained.

"Sarah loves her grandmother dearly and we thought it would be good for her to spend as much time with her as possible," Lawrence interjected while placing his empty glass on a table next to his chair.

"How is your son, Benjamin?," Caroline asked. "I'm sure he is growing into a fine young man. I hear he has recently returned from England," she added.

"Oh, yes! We are so glad to have him home after being gone for a little over two years," Rebecca exclaimed. "His grandfather thought it would be a good experience for him to be educated in England as it would make him a more well-rounded individual. John and I were just saying the other day we cannot believe Benjamin will be twenty-one after the new year," she continued.

"Our children are growing up quickly," John said. "Does that mean we are getting old?," he continued with a laugh.

"Speak for yourself!," Rebecca protested with a complacent smile which caused Caroline and Lawrence to laugh along with John even louder.

As the two couples continued to happily converse by the fire, a house servant duly appeared to inform Lawrence that the Thompson's trunk had been delivered to their room.

"Let us show you to your room," Caroline politely said. "I'm sure you two would like to rest a bit before supper," Caroline continued as they all arose from their seats.

Lawrence and Caroline escorted their guests upstairs to ensure they had everything they needed for a comfortable stay. As they entered the room, a maid was completing her final inspection. After receiving a smile and a nod from Caroline, the servant politely left the room. When they received confirmation that John and Rebecca were pleased, Lawrence and Caroline turned to leave. Before closing the door on their way out, Caroline confirmed the time that supper would be served in the dining room. A short time later, after resting an hour due to their arduous trip, John and Rebecca rejoined their hosts for a delicious supper. After a leisurely meal with good food and more conversation, the foursome decided to retire early for the evening in anticipation of the spectacular event that was to take place the following evening.

The next day, Caroline and Rebecca were in a constant whirlwind making sure their gowns were freshened and their elegant accessories were properly coordinated in hopes of making an impressive appearance at the ball. Lawrence and John spent a less stressful day relaxing in the parlor talking politics, enjoying brandy and smoking their pipes.

Later that evening, as Caroline sat on the stool in front of her vanity in their upstairs bedchamber, Lawrence stood behind her while he tied the ribbon of her favorite pearl necklace at the nape of her neck. After continuing to gaze into the looking glass and admire the final touches of her elegant attire, Caroline satisfactorily concluded that she was pleased with her appearance as a smile slowly appeared across her face.

"Caroline, have I told you lately how beautiful you are," Lawrence said with admiration as he stared at his wife's reflection.

"Thank you, dear," Caroline said as she returned his affection. "You know that you are my knight in shining armor," she playfully added as she arose from the seat of her vanity and walked toward one of the windows that overlooked the Palace Green in front of the house. "It looks as if the guests are beginning to arrive," Caroline continued as she saw a procession of coaches making their way northward down Palace Street toward the Governor's Palace. "We certainly don't want to be late!"

"I'm ready, dear," Lawrence replied. "I'm sure John and Rebecca are downstairs waiting for us in the parlor," he continued while standing near the bedchamber door.

"After you, my lady," Lawrence politely said as he opened the door for his wife.

As the handsome couple walked into the upstairs hallway and descended the stairs to join their friends in the front parlor, their striking appearance created an image of aristocracy and anyone watching could have easily mistaken them for royalty. Caroline wore a beautiful gold-colored silk ball gown, with cascades of off-white ruffles at the edge of the sleeves, and her beautiful brown hair piled high on her head was accentuated with stands of cream-colored pearls. Lawrence was equally impressive in a green embroidered silk tailcoat with matching britches, white stockings and sparkling jewels set in the buckles of his shoes.

"Well, don't you two look just like a king and queen," Rebecca said as Lawrence and Caroline gracefully entered through the parlor door.

"We could say the same about you two!," Caroline returned the compliment as she admired John and Rebecca's elegant evening attire.

"Yes, you two ladies are a vision of loveliness," John said to flatter the ladies.

"I'll second that motion," Lawrence replied while both ladies flashed an appreciative smile. "The coach is waiting out front," Lawrence continued while he and John began to assist Caroline and Rebecca with their capes.

As they turned to leave, a servant standing quietly at the entrance bowed as he opened the door for the four of them.

"Thank you, Lucius," Lawrence replied to his faithful servant.

After they boarded the waiting shiny black coach, with its fancy gold letter "E" inscribed on the door, Amos – the Eldridge's driver – steered the horses southward down the west side of Palace Street toward Duke of Gloucester Street in order to loop around on the east side of Palace

Street. As their coach began to turn into the east side of the street after circling around the south end of the Palace Green, another approaching coach slowed to allow the driver to enter the street ahead of them to continue northward toward the Governor's Palace. While the Eldridge's elegant and familiar coach continued northward in the procession of arriving guests, the Governor's Palace could be seen off in the distance through the leafless trees that lined the edge of the Palace Green. In the early winter evening sky, flickering candles illuminated the windows of the tall lantern cupola that crowned the flat balustraded roof of the stately palace that had been placed there to signal the spectacular event.

"It seems the governor is certainly trying to make a grand impression with his first Christmas gala," Caroline said while being mesmerized by the flickering light in the distance as she gazed out the window of the coach.

"Yes, my dear. I hear it will be an event to remember," Lawrence replied.

"I hear his wine cellar is one of the best!," Rebecca said as she turned her head to glance at her husband sitting beside her.

"I hear he is excessively acquisitive," John replied in reference to the rumors of Lord Dunmore's greed and desire for material possessions.

"I have also heard rumors of his philandering!," Caroline said.

"Well, let's hope his wife and family join him soon to put those rumors to rest," Rebecca said while Lawrence and John looked at each other in amusement as they listened to their wives.

As the arriving coaches approached their destination, they gradually entered the circular loop in front of the palace. The drivers patiently waited their turn as they slowed and stopped several times before delivering their passengers at the front entrance. The brick wall that surrounded the palace curved outward to allow stately iron-grilled entrance gates to welcome its guests. The brick columns on each side of the gates were topped by the British lion and unicorn and supported an elaborately scrolled heading that hung overhead. Festive garland of pine and boxwood draped the brick columned posts and two large wreaths decorated with fruit and berries had been hung from the iron-grilled entrance gates.

When the Eldridge's coach came to a stop in front of the gates, Lawrence and John quickly exited while turning to extend their hands outward to assist their wives as they stepped out of the coach. Once they had safely exited, Amos quickly drove onward to the carriage house and stables on the west side of the palace so the next coach could let its passengers depart at the front entrance.

Once Lawrence and John escorted their wives through the iron gates, they were greeted by a formally landscaped forecourt on each side of the central walkway that led to the palace's front entrance. Luminous lanterns had been periodically placed on each side of the walkway and the glowing flames led the way to the merriment that awaited inside.

"Oh, how festive!," Rebecca exclaimed as she admired the radiance of the lanterns as they strolled along the walkway toward the entrance door.

"It is quite an impressive welcome. The palace is quite impressive too," John replied as his wife looped her arm in his while they continued down the walkway and looked upward at the building in front of them.

The palace rose two full stories to a denticulated cornice and was topped by a dormered hip roof that supported the balustraded platform and tall lantern cupola that could be seen during their arrival. When guests reached the simple square-transomed doorway beneath a wrought-iron balcony, they were welcomed by manservants who attended to their coats before being escorted to the ballroom at the rear of the palace.

As guests entered the ballroom, a reception line began to form as Lord Dunmore welcomed his guests while standing beneath the full-length oil portraits of Queen Charlotte and King George III that hung on each side of the large interior double entrance doors. After receiving a royal welcome by the governor, guests began to mingle while attendants descended the room to serve wine and spirits amongst the chatter of voices as guests began to form in groups to engage in conversation. A large crystal punch bowl sat on a table in one corner of the room for those who preferred a drink with a little less potency. In another corner of the room, a sextet of musicians was seated in a group while anxiously awaiting a signal from Lord Dunmore to begin playing their instruments.

"I think of father when I am in this room," Caroline fondly said when they walked through the doorway while remembering her father's involvement with the addition of the ballroom that took place almost two decades earlier.

"It certainly is a splendid room!," Rebecca said as she admired the elaborate dentil crown molding, high ceilings and large wooden pediments that surmounted the two doorways on each side of the room.

"The exterior is just as impressive. The double entrance doors at the rear overlook the palace gardens. There is also a wood-carved, gaily painted royal arms of the first King Georges hanging outside over the doorway," Lawrence elaborated.

"Father was so proud of his accomplishment. I was a young girl in my early twenties and Lawrence and I had not long been married," Caroline said with a happy look on her face. "That was years ago but it almost seems like yesterday," she continued while her thoughts traveled back in time.

While Caroline's wandering mind lingered a few moments in the past, she was quickly brought back to the present as the sextet of musicians began to play their violins, cellos, harpsichord and flute. As Caroline watched the colony's gentry in their elegant attire begin to form a "Z" pattern in the center of the ballroom floor to dance the minuet, her observation served as a vivid reminder that an invitation to the Governor's Palace was an honor of distinction. Only the aristocracy of the colony, prominent political figures, planters of Virginia and the gentry of Williamsburg were granted the privilege of attending such an event.

Lawrence and John soon led Caroline and Rebecca into the center of the ballroom floor to join the other merry couples. Bystanders eagerly watched the dancers rise onto the ball of their foot on certain beats and drop their heel almost to the floor on others, while maintaining an effort that required balance, concentration, and unspoken communication with one's partner. Other fancy dances followed, after those who wished to perform the minuet had done so.

"I am surprised to see Alexander here," John said as the couples returned to the side of the room after leaving the dance floor.

"Yes, I noticed him dancing. I'm sure that he is here by the invitation of a wealthy female patron," Lawrence cynically said while he pulled a handkerchief from his coat pocket.

"Did you overexert yourself, dear? That certainly was a rigorous dance, wasn't it?," Caroline said to her husband with a laugh while she noticed him wiping the perspiration from his forehead.

"I don't think it is so much the dancing as it is Lord Dunmore's cast iron stove working overtime tonight," he teasingly replied while referring to the decorative black cast iron Abraham Buzaglo heating stove on the other side of the room.

"Who is Alexander with?," Rebecca asked Caroline after her and Lawrence's playful exchange.

"She is the wealthy Miriam Hathaway," Caroline replied. "She inherited a large estate when her husband passed away a year ago," she added.

"She does look a little older than Alexander," Rebecca assessed.

"Alexander was her late husband's lawyer," Lawrence informed.

"I'm sure he's only with her because he's using her to his benefit," John replied. "There is something about Alexander that I have never trusted, especially since Simon Bartram's trial. I've always had a gut feeling that he was somehow involved with Simon's illegal business dealings," John confided to Lawrence.

"I've had those same feelings," Lawrence agreed with a feeling of unease as he looked across the room at Alexander and Miriam looking back at them.

Anger and bitterness burned within Alexander as he noticed the stares of the two men and their wives from across the room. His jealousy seemed to always get the better of him, especially when he was in their presence. Alexander felt inferior to their aristocratic backgrounds and believed their success was simply attained by being part of the gentry of Virginia. He believed these men were given success due to their station in life, unlike his struggle to work hard for everything he got. Alexander's deep resentment drove him to defeat these men in the courtroom and when he was not able to do so, his temper raged and his blood boiled. Although, Alexander knew that it was more advantageous to keep your friends close and your enemies even closer by masking his true feelings and hiding his real demeanor. However,

Alexander never realized, or would ever admit, that most of his losses were due to his own dishonesty, immorality and unethical values.

Although Alexander was not from a privileged background, he was able to obtain a decent education as a young boy and by fortunate luck to be educated at the College of William and Mary. A wealthy great uncle, who achieved his fortune from questionable sources, served as Alexander's benefactor. Alexander's mother eagerly accepted her uncle's financial favors for the sake of herself and her son. Alexander had been conceived when passion ignited between his mother and a sailor who was temporarily in port. The sailor eventually departed to sea and never returned. Alexander's great uncle took pity on his unwed niece and her son by providing financial means while she turned her head to the true source of the funds. When Alexander grew into a young man and eventually attended the college with the upper-class society of Virginia, he realized more than ever before that he would never be part of the gentry of Virginia due to his less fortunate background. However, he soon learned that his handsome looks – a tall athletic build, masculine appeal, striking black hair and charming ways – could easily be used to his advantage, especially with the ladies.

While Alexander led Miriam to the center of the room to dance the minuet, his mind was elsewhere as he imagined being in the passionate embrace of his current lover. As the sexual image formed in his mind a smile appeared on Alexander's face and when Miriam looked at her handsome escort she mistakenly assumed his smile was for her. Alexander used Miriam, or anyone else he could use to achieve what he wanted, as a means to an end. Besides his sum for handling her legal affairs, Miriam provided a way to associate with the elite social class of the colony while allowing Alexander to move in the circles of his and his lover's soon to be victims.

Alexander was handsome and charismatic and extraordinarily devious when hiding his true nature from the people he charmed. Anyone watching him at the ball would never guess that he was displaying a false façade and that his thoughts were somewhere else.

Alexander's younger lover's sensuous aura, fair skin and dark brown hair, that he remembered so well when he first met her when she was as a teenager, had now years later developed into an undeniable sexual appeal and her sultry looks were irresistible to his lustful desires. Alexander remembered Simon Bartram's daughter as if it were yesterday and if she had been older when they had first met, he knew they would have been lovers then. Alexander and Simon's daughter had been in each other's presence on numerous occasions when he was involved with her father's illegal dealings. There was an obvious sexual tension between the two, but due to her young age and Alexander's mistaken sense of her innocence, he never crossed over those boundaries.

After Simon Bartram was tried and convicted, Alexander was forced to distance himself from that situation for fear of being discovered. He and Simon's partnership created financial gain for himself and also benefited Simon by helping him evade the law. When Simon's illicit dealings were finally discovered, Alexander fought to prove Simon's innocence in the courtroom but failed. When the case was over and Simon's daughter's situation was determined, Alexander temporarily lost touch with the sultry girl that still remained in his thoughts. Being underage and having no means of financial support, Simon's daughter was placed in the care of guardians. She was constantly passed from one family to another, due to her difficult attitude and her resentful personality.

Revenge on the two men that sealed her father's fate consumed her thoughts through her teenage years and she vowed to carry out her plan if it was the last thing she did on this earth. John Thompson and Lawrence Eldridge's names would be embedded in her memory for ever.

When Simon's daughter was placed with her last foster family in Fredericksburg before coming of age in 1768, she had finally learned that controlling her anger and resentment and replacing it with trickery and deceit would better serve her in achieving her true intentions. She appeared so sweet and caring to her new family and was so crafty at doing so that the couple wondered why they were warned of her unruliness before taking her in. Her new guardians welcomed her into their home but didn't waste any time placing her on a daily schedule of chores. As part of her responsibilities, she would regularly ride in the wagon with her foster father to pick-up farming supplies at the waterfront. While waiting in the wagon as he tended to business, she occasionally overheard men talking and discretely eavesdropped on their conversations.

One night, after learning about the popular gambling spots in the town from her eavesdropping, she secretly slipped out her bedroom window to explore. Once she had dressed herself to appear older and enhanced her sensual appeal, she set out for a night of fun. When she entered the smoke-filled room at a warehouse on the waterfront, she was immediately drawn to a handsome man at the tables. His dark hair and debonair manner instantly stirred something within her. After casually mingling around the room and making subtle inquiries, she quickly learned his name was Francis Beckham. After Francis made a big win at the tables, she seductively introduced herself and offered to help him celebrate. While rambling in a drunken state during their passionate encounter, she learned that he was from the well-known Beckhams of King George County in the northern part of the colony. However, she also discovered that he was considered the black sheep of their aristocratic family. His constant gambling was an embarrassment to his parents and his brothers but his younger sister, Marie, always idolized her older brother and his charming ways. Ironically, Francis realized that this beautiful young woman that he had recently met resembled his sister in looks but not in personality. However, the plotting mind of Simon's daughter saw this situation with Francis Beckham as a financial opportunity to help her escape the miserable life she had lived for the past few years and to move a step closer toward her eventual goal.

She and Francis regularly frolicked during his visits to Fredericksburg and one night after an ardent meeting, she cunningly claimed she was with child. After initial opposition from his family because of her questionable background, Francis agreed to marry her since she was carrying his child and heir. Once they settled in as man and wife at the Beckham estate, their relationship soon deteriorated when he discovered her true deceitful and difficult personality. The personality of the sweet loving person that he originally met had disappeared.

Once he discovered she was truly not with child, he vehemently demanded an annulment of their union. As she became enraged, a violent physical argument ensued at the top of the stairs and after a short struggle she pushed Francis backwards down the steps. She looked down the stairwell at his limp body and ran down the steps to examine his condition. Once she determined the fall had taken his life, she secretly smiled assuming his death would secure her a financial future. The Beckham family, after learning about her connection to the infamous Simon Bartram and for fear of gossip and scandal that would permanently blemish their family name, aggressively fought her claim to Francis' share of their estate. Since she had no monetary means to legally fight them, she reluctantly agreed on a large settlement of money and signed away any rights for future claims.

Even though Francis's beloved sister Marie never met her brother's underhanded wife, since she herself was married and living near Williamsburg with her older aristocratic husband, she was shocked when she learned of the chain of events surrounding her brother's death. After hearing her family's suspicions regarding Francis's death, she was constantly plagued with wanting to know the truth. Even with the comfort of her husband, she still agonized over her dear beloved brother's death and promised herself that one day she would discover the truth behind his suspicious demise.

While gradually discovering her desirability to the opposite sex, Simon's daughter now became even more confident and knew she could use her womanly allure to her advantage. After her ordeal with the Beckhams, she decided to try her luck in the southern part of the colony where she knew she would be unknown. When traveling south by coach to Williamsburg, she caught the eye of a mature wealthy merchant traveler who was returning home from a business trip in Richmond. After accepting his immediate advances, it wasn't long before she lured him into marriage and was living on the outskirts of Williamsburg. Not long after settling into their married life, her new husband mysteriously died from a tragic fall.

Not long after being "widowed" a second time and while continuing on her quest for revenge, Simon's now wealthy daughter crossed paths with Alexander Drake once again. One day, during the summer of 1771 when shopping in Williamsburg, she recognized a familiar face as she glanced across the street while strolling down the sidewalk. She instantly recognized the handsome and worldly man who had captivated her attention as a young girl. Even for her strong physical attraction to Alexander, she looked at their reunion as a fortunate opportunity to use him. She knew that Alexander could be useful with her plan of revenge but could never bring her the status, respectability and wealth that she so deeply desired in life.

Simon Bartram's daughter and Alexander Drake's equal hatred of both men came together in a common goal. She wanted to harm Lawrence Eldridge and John Thompson in a way that would bring them the severe pain that she felt when they convicted her father and left her penniless. Alexander, on the other hand, experienced constant defeat and humiliation in the courtroom when up against both men and was resentful because he wasn't born into a better station in life. Once Simon's daughter realized the physical power she had over Alexander, she easily seduced him into her web of revenge. With her disguised false promises for a future together, Alexander felt compelled to do her biding so he could be with this seductive female who had captivated him under her spell. Alexander had no idea that Simon's daughter was only using him for her own purpose.

As the dance at the Governor's Christmas Ball ended, the sound of clapping hands and excited voices reminded Alexander where he was. While he and Miriam left the center of the floor to mingle with a small group on the other side of the room, his mind began to focus on the vengeful task he was sent to the ball to accomplish.

"How would you ladies like to take another turn on the dance floor," Lawrence said while smiling at Caroline and Rebecca when he noticed that Alexander and Miriam had finished their dance.

"We would love to!," Caroline answered for both she and Rebecca as Lawrence and John took their wives hands to lead them to the center of the room.

After a lengthy period of dancing, merriment and socializing with friends and associates, Lord Dunmore announced dinner would be served in the formal dining room. The governor's exceptionally long table was set with the finest linen, silver, and china and his food was delicious and his wines were excellent. Food was carried to the formal dining room from the kitchen dependency through the service area west of the mansion. Beef, mutton, turkey and pork, along with cheese, apples and nuts, were served in abundance while everyone enjoyed a feast fit for a king. The meal was brought to an end with a variety of cakes, plum pudding, custards and mince meat pies.

As everyone began to leave their place at the long table that had been arranged to accommodate all the attendees of the ball, Lord Dunmore announced there would be more dancing in the ballroom. While everyone returned to the ballroom to enjoy several more rounds of dancing and lighthearted social mingling, the musicians enthusiastically took their seats and began to play.

"It seems Alexander has abandoned Miriam," Caroline said as she saw the widow standing alone in the corner.

"He's probably somewhere charming another pretty lady," Rebecca sarcastically replied.

"Yes, that does sound like him," Lawrence said with a laugh as he looked at John smiling in agreement.

The men led their wives to the center of the room to enjoy another round of dancing. After returning to the side of the room to enjoy a few more drinks and conversation, they eventually noticed the crowd had gotten thinner.

"It looks like people are beginning to leave," Rebecca said, although noticing that Alexander had rejoined Miriam on the other side of the room.

"Are you ladies ready to retire for the evening?," John asked when he noticed Caroline discreetly yawning.

"I'm ready whenever you all are," Caroline responded as they all came to an agreement that it was time to leave.

"I'll arrange for the coach to be brought around front," Lawrence informed as he turned to walk toward one of the servants standing against the wall nearby.

After the driver pulled the coach around to the front entrance gates, the foursome hurriedly moved along the walkway and quickly boarded their coach to escape the chilly night air.

"It has turned rather cold this evening," Caroline said as she stepped into the coach and relaxed on the comfortable leather seat.

"It will be nice to get home and sit by the fire," Lawrence replied as he sat beside her.

"What an enjoyable evening!," Rebecca said while she and John eased into the carriage seats facing them. "Although, I'm exhausted!," she added while remembering their several rounds of rigorous dancing.

"We are not used to dancing," John replied with a teasing smile. "We should all sleep good tonight!" he added as the coach began to make its way around the loop in front of the palace.

As the driver drove the horses down the west side of Palace Street toward Hemsworth House, the passengers sat quietly in their seats for the remainder of the short ride. Just as they began to relax, the sound of an exploding gunshot blasted through the silence. The terrified horses suddenly bolted ahead causing the carriage to violently jerk and sway while the screaming voices of Rebecca and Caroline frightened them even more. As the driver failed to calm the horses, they continued running out of control as the carriage careened over the edge of the street and onto the Palace Green.

"Oh, my God!," Lawrence exclaimed as he saw Amos fly off the driver's seat and land on the ground.

As the horses broke free from coach, the coach continued weaving wildly ahead as the ladies continued to scream in horror. As John held tightly to the window frame, his eyes widened in horror as he saw the rear wheel suddenly wobble off its axle. More loud screams of terror could be heard from inside the coach as the ladies were thrown from one side to the other as the coach toppled on its side to the ground. Lawrence and John tightly held on to the window frames to prevent themselves from falling on top of their wives.

"Are you all okay?," the driver yelled as he painfully limped toward the overturned coach.

Lawrence barely heard him as he and John scrambled to determine if everyone was safe.

"Are you okay?," Amos anxiously called out once again as he reached the coach and flung open the door.

"I think so, Amos!," Lawrence replied as John reached for Amos' hand to be helped out of the coach.

Lawrence remained in the coach as he assisted the ladies from behind while John and Amos pulled them safely from the overturned carriage. Once everyone stood securely on the ground in relief, they once again confirmed everyone's well-being with the exception of a few scratches and bruises.

"We won't worry about the horses tonight. We'll look for them in the morning," Lawrence determined. "We can't do anything about the coach either," he added.

"I'll help you take care of everything in the morning," John replied.

"Mr. Lawrence, me and my son Jonah will get up at daybreak and go look for the horses," Amos informed.

"Thank you, Amos. That would be very much appreciated," Lawrence replied as he placed his hand on Amos's shoulder. "Are you sure you are okay? It looks like you suffered the most harm," Lawrence continued while noticing Amos's torn britches and his slight limp.

"I'm fine, Mr. Lawrence," Amos replied. "I'm sure it's just a mild sprain. Can you all make it back to the house okay?," Amos asked.

"We are fine," Rebecca confirmed as Caroline nodded in agreement while they tried to regain their composure.

While everyone wandered in a daze across the Palace Green toward Hemsworth House, the disheveled passengers bore no resemblance to the elegantly dressed gentry that had just attended the Governor's Ball. As they entered the front door and climbed the stairs in the front entrance hall to retire to their rooms, they silently pondered over the traumatic incident and were relieved that they had all escaped unharmed.

The following morning when the hazy fog that had blanketed the town during the night began to dissipate, Amos and his son Jonah left in search of the horses. Lawrence and John set out across the street toward the Palace Green to assess the damage to the coach caused by the disturbing event that had occurred the previous evening. As they walked through the skid marks across the disheveled ground and approached the coach lying on its side, both men felt a sigh of relief as they recalled the harrowing experience.

"Wow, this looks worse than it did last night!," Lawrence said as he leaned into the doorway of the coach. "What a mess!," he added as he saw the damage that had occurred inside.

"Look at this axle! It's a miracle that none of us were killed!," John exclaimed as he saw the bare axle sticking out of the coach.

"Isn't that the truth!," Lawrence replied.

"I wonder how the horses broke free?," John asked as he pointed to the harness straps lying in a heap on the ground in front of the coach.

Both men squatted down on their ankles to examine the pile of leather still partially attached to the front of the damaged coach lying on its side.

"Look here! It's obvious they were cut with a knife," Lawrence said while holding one of the straps in his hand. "That gunshot must have been planned to spook the horses," he deduced.

"It certainly appears that way, doesn't it?," John replied in bewilderment while both men stared at the straps in disbelief before rising and stepping back to look at the whole scene.

"Yes, and it also appears that this wheel was purposely loosened," Lawrence said as he walked nearer to the coach and bent over to examine the rear axle sticking out its side. "We were lucky to escape unscathed," he said to confirm John's earlier comment while glancing at the loose wheel lying on the ground a few yards from the coach.

"I wonder who could be responsible for this?," John responded with uncertainty while he scanned his memory trying to think of anyone who could have a grudge against him or his family.

"I was thinking the same thing," Lawrence wondered out loud as both men stood looking at each other in confusion.

After returning to the house, Lawrence and John hesitated telling their wives what they had discovered while they all sat down by the fire in the front parlor.

"I can't imagine who would do this to us!," Rebecca responded with fear as they all looked at each other in shock.

Several minutes of silence ensued as they all sat quietly in their seats as their minds wondered who could have done such a thing.

"I am just so thankful we were not injured!," Caroline calmly exclaimed as she broke the silence in the room.

"Yes, thank God we were spared any harm," Lawrence replied in relief.

"I concur!," John said as he quickly rose from his seat to walk toward the fireplace. "This a dangerous situation!," he exclaimed with agitation.

Lawrence and Caroline looked at John in shock while realizing they had never seen this side to his normally quiet and composed nature.

"You are welcome to stay with us as long as you need to recover from this awful ordeal," Caroline offered as she glanced at Rebecca and John in hopes of calming him down.

"Yes, please do," Lawrence confirmed.

"We appreciate your hospitality but we are anxious to return home," Rebecca replied.

"It will be the first time in more than two years since our family has been together at Christmas," John said with anticipation.

"It's hard to believe that Christmas is only a week away!," Caroline responded in an attempt to continue to lighten the atmosphere.

"We are so thankful to have Benjamin back with us!," Rebecca said with excitement. "We are looking forward to our celebration on Christmas Day!," she added.

Early the next morning, John and Rebecca waved goodbye as their own coach pulled away from the brick walkway in front of Hemsworth House. They were full of anticipation to return to their home and spend Christmas with their newly reunited family. However, the thought of the horrendous incident that nearly took their lives severely lingered in their minds.

GARY ROWE

Chapter 7

The next day, during late afternoon, the Thompson's coach entered the iron gates to the Atherton estate. John and Rebecca were relieved to reach the safety of their familiar surroundings. During their two-day return trip to Atherton County, they were still in disbelief of what had happened in Williamsburg and had no idea who could have caused such an evil act that had nearly taken their lives.

When the coach pulled in front of the brick steps to the front entrance of their home, Benjamin and Robert were eagerly awaiting their return.

"Welcome home, you two! So, how was the ball?," Robert asked his daughter and son-in-law as he and Benjamin stepped out of the front door and onto the porch while Horace trailed behind them happily wagging his tail.

"It was quite an event!," Rebecca replied to her father as John helped her step out of the coach. "Although, we had a harrowing experience when we left the ball," she fretted while recalling the awful incident as Benjamin ran down the steps to greet his parents with Horace at his heels.

"What happened?," Benjamin asked as he noticed the look of fear on his mother's face while he hugged her and kissed her on the cheek.

"We'll tell you all about it a little later," John said to temporarily avoid the subject while Benjamin turned to hug him.

"Okay, father," Benjamin replied while an expression of curiosity appeared on his face.

"Hey there, boy! Did you miss us while we were away?," John playfully asked Horace while he bent forward to pet the canine on his head as the canine happily looked up at him.

"We are glad you made it home safely," Benjamin replied while deferring his curiosity as they turned to climb the steps to join Robert on the porch.

"I'm sure you two would like to rest after your journey," Robert said as Rebecca hugged her father and John shook his hand.

"It was a tiring trip but we have been so eager to return home and enjoy Christmas with you!," Rebecca happily replied as she affectionately smiled at her father.

When they entered the entrance hall, Rebecca immediately noticed the festive greenery that had been draped along the banister rail from the second-floor landing down to the newel post in the foyer.

"We thought we would surprise you!," Benjamin said as he watched the expression of excitement appear on his mother's face.

"It's beautiful!," Rebecca exclaimed as she admired their handiwork.

"Grandfather and I went out early this morning and gathered magnolia leaves, pine and boxwood," Benjamin proudly said. "We decorated the mantles too! We were glad we finished before you got home," he added.

"It's lovely!," Rebecca fondly smiled at her son as they walked into the front parlor. "It will make Christmas all the more special!," she continued while noticing the greenery that had been draped across the mantle.

"I just wish your mother Elizabeth could be here with us," Robert said to Rebecca as thoughts of his beloved wife entered his mind.

As John and Rebecca sat down on the sofa and Benjamin and Robert in the wing chairs that were arranged near the fireplace, Horace found a comfortable spot on the floor nearer to Benjamin.

"I still miss her so much," Rebecca said as she remembered her beautiful mother and the happy Christmas's the three of them shared during her childhood.

"That is why we must appreciate the time we have together and make the most of our time here on earth," Robert reflected.

"I can't agree more, Robert!," John replied to his father-in-law's wisdom. "That is why we are so glad that Benjamin is back with us!," he continued as he turned his head to smile at his son.

"Well, I am glad to be home!," Benjamin happily replied. "I enjoyed my experiences in England but I am so happy to be back with my family," he added.

"So, what happened in Williamsburg?," Robert asked while remembering his daughter's comment when they first arrived.

"When we were leaving the ball, it appears that someone purposely frightened the horses," Rebecca recalled with fear. "And the coach overturned!," she added as a look of shock appeared on Benjamin and Robert's faces.

After John and Rebecca explained in detail their horrifying experience that had nearly taken their lives, Robert and Benjamin could hardly believe what they had just heard.

"When we went to assess the damage the following morning, we discovered the horses' harnesses had been cut with a knife," John added.

"Do you have any idea who would do such a thing?," Robert asked with serious concern.

"No, I have tried but cannot think of anyone. Although, it could be directed at either Lawrence or myself," John said. "We do sometimes make enemies in our profession," he added.

"We also saw Alexander Drake at the ball," Rebecca unpleasantly said.

"Isn't he the lawyer who defended that famous traitor Simon Bartram a few years ago?," Robert asked as he recalled the well-known trial.

"Yes, and you know how I feel about Alexander. He is someone who cannot be trusted," John seriously answered.

"Well, grandfather and I are so relieved that you both were not harmed!," Benjamin replied.

"We are blessed to be safely reunited and we should make the most of our Christmas celebration!," Robert exclaimed while admiring his family around him.

During the few remaining days that followed until Christmas arrived, Rebecca busily managed the kitchen staff as they prepared the delicious food they would enjoy on Christmas Day. She and John had planned a small celebration with their family and a few close friends from nearby Atherton Village. Rebecca wanted everything to be perfect and meticulously planned every detail. Robert, John and Benjamin spent their time discussing plans for expanding their tobacco crop and making improvements to the plantation in the coming year.

While they all relaxed by the fire in the front parlor on Christmas Eve, and Horace found his usual place on the floor next to Benjamin, they were in great anticipation of celebrating the birthday of their Savior.

"We have a busy day ahead of us tomorrow!," Rebecca said with excitement.

"I am looking forward to worshiping with my family," Robert said. "Christmas morning Mass was so special to your mother, Elizabeth," Robert reminded Rebecca.

"I wish I had been fortunate to know her," Benjamin thoughtfully said as he looked at his mother and grandfather.

"She would have loved you as well," Rebecca fondly responded.

"I think your mother and I will retire for the evening since we have a full day tomorrow," John said to Benjamin and Robert as he and Rebecca arose from the sofa while their movement caused Horace to raise his head off the floor and look at them.

"Benjamin and I will be up shortly," Robert replied.

After John and Rebecca climbed the stairs and began to walk down the upstairs hallway, John romantically reached for Rebecca's hand. No words were spoken as they walked hand-in-hand to their bedchamber. When John closed the door behind them, he turned to Rebecca and gently placed his hands on her shoulders as he stood facing her.

"I love you Rebecca. You are the love of my life and I was truly blessed the day I met you," John affectionately said. "I know I don't tell you enough," he continued while he looked deeply in her eyes as he raised his right hand to gently touch her on the cheek.

"John, I hope you have no doubt that I feel the same way about you," Rebecca lovingly replied before they shared an intimate kiss.

"Never doubt my love for you and Benjamin." John softly replied after his lips left hers while he continued to gaze into her eyes.

"I almost feel guilty for being so happy," Rebecca said with an adoring smile.

"I am so thankful we have our whole lives ahead of us," John affectionately responded as they turned toward their bed in hopes of a peaceful night.

As the stillness of the night came over the Thompson household and the early morning hours approached, John was suddenly awakened from a sound sleep. As he slowly opened his eyes and looked up at the ceiling, he initially thought he was dreaming. When John realized he heard a strange sound, his body slightly tensed but he remained perfectly still while trying to determine what it was. As he continued to lie in bed, he thought he heard the sound of a closing door. Then he heard footsteps. When John shifted in bed, Rebecca began to stir when she sensed his movement beside her.

"What is it, John?," Rebecca groggily said as she rolled over on her side in their mahogany four poster bed to look over her shoulder at her husband.

"I thought I heard a strange noise coming from downstairs," John said as he slightly raised himself up on his right arm to look at his wife.

"I wonder who it could be?," Rebecca wondered out loud as she rolled on her side a little more closer to John.

"I'm not sure. The servants shouldn't be in the house at this time of night," he said while continuing to stay alert to see if he could hear the noise again. "I think I'll go see what it is," he informed as he began to slip out of bed.

"Be careful, dear," Rebecca whispered to John as his feet met the floor.

As he stood and reached to light the candle in the chamberstick that sat on top of the chest of drawers beside the bed, he turned to his wife and gazed into her eyes to ease her fears.

"Don't worry, my love. I'll be back in a few minutes," John softly said.

"Be careful, John," Rebecca whispered once again as she watched him disappear through the doorway into the dark upstairs hall chamber.

As John made his way down the hallway and then slowly and quietly descended the steps into the front entrance hall, he tightly held the handle of the chamberstick while he raised his arm higher to allow the flame to reflect more light around him. As he silently continued down the steps, the flickering candle cast eerie shadows as the light reflected off objects in the hallway below. When John stepped off the last step and into the entrance hall, he saw Horace standing perfectly still in shadows toward the back of the hallway. As the candlelight reflected off Horace's exposed teeth, the animal began to slowly growl as he peered into the darkness.

"What is it, boy? It's just me," John said to Horace as he began to relax while the dog continued to softly growl and stare past him into the darkness.

All of the sudden, a hooded figure appeared out of the shadows and lunged at John from behind. The chamberstick immediately flew out of John's hand and landed upright on the floor beside the window near the front door. As the candle flickered near the edge of the drapery fabric that touched the floor, the flame caught the edge of the material as it began to ignite. While John struggled to turn and face his attacker, Horace immediately darted towards them. As both men began to wildly swing at each other with their fists, Horace's growling grew louder as he leaped through the air with an open jaw and landed beside them as they fell to the floor. While both figures furiously wrestled on the floor in an attempt to overpower the other, fists continued to fly as the struggle ensued.

As the curtains became fully engulfed with flames, a piece of the burning fabric fell off and landed on the rug in the hallway. Horace steadily tried to bite the attacker as the animal lunged at him with his sharp teeth. The attacker attempted to push the dog away with one hand as he punched John with his other fist. After several rounds of violent punches, the attacker gave John a harmful blow to his head. As John's body lie perfectly still on the floor, Horace continued to ferociously growl as his teeth latched onto the hooded man's forearm.

Smoked filled the air as flames spread throughout the hallway and began to overtake anything that would burn. While Horace violently jerked at the buttoned fabric around the edge of the attacker's sleeve, a piece of the fabric ripped off near his gloved hand. As Horace slightly fell backwards while the tearing fabric separated from the rest of garment, the hooded man quickly rose from the floor and stumbled through the smoke-filled room and hurriedly rushed out the front door.

While the hallway continued go up in flames, Horace began to whimper and nudge John's lifeless body with his nose to try and arouse him. Once the animal began to lick his face, John slowly began to regain consciousness as he gradually became aware of his dangerous surroundings. While he began to awkwardly rise from the floor, John stumbled but caught the newel post at the foot of the stairs with his hand to prevent himself from falling back to the floor.

Rebecca and Benjamin suddenly appeared at the top of the upstairs landing. As they struggled to see through the smoke-filled air and called out to see if anyone was there, they frantically rushed down the stairs when they heard John's panic-stricken voice.

"We must get outdoors!," John said to his wife and son as they reached the bottom of the stairs and rushed to his side.

"Father, are you okay?," Benjamin asked as a look of fear overcame him.

"John, what happened?," Rebecca frantically asked.

"Someone attacked me from behind. But we must get out of the house! Now!," John fearfully said once again as he began to usher them toward the front door.

As they made their way through the smoke and flames, Horace continued to bark as they rushed toward the front door.

"Where is father!," Rebecca hysterically gasped as she quickly turned to John.

"He must be upstairs!," John replied in a panic-stricken voice as they stopped at the front door.

"Oh, John!," Rebecca said as John turned to go after her father.

John quickly stopped in his tracks and turned back to look deeply into his wife's eyes before quickly turning to his son and affectionately squeezing Benjamin's shoulder.

"Ben, take care of your mother!," John exclaimed before turning to race up the stairs while dodging the flames along the way.

Benjamin quickly took his mother by the arm to lead her outside. After rushing down the brick steps, they staggered across the front lawn until they were a safe distance away from the burning house. Benjamin and Rebecca watched in horror as smoke billowed out through the door and flames flared from the surrounding windows. As they watched the horrendous scene, tears of disbelief flowed when they began to realize they may never see John and Robert alive again.

Suddenly, voices could be heard from behind as Benjamin and Rebecca turned to see several servants running toward the house and shouting as they carried buckets of water they had retrieved from the nearby well in the back of the house. After getting as close to the house as possible to throw water on the crackling flames in hope of extinguishing the fire, they quickly returned to refill their buckets and courageously continued the routine until they tearfully realized their efforts were hopeless.

As Rebecca frantically sobbed and screamed in the comfort of her son's arms, she painfully imagined her brave husband and loving father in the burning inferno as a servant gently placed a blanket around her shoulders. Rebecca's heart severely ached as it had never before in her forty-seven years.

When the sun rose in the morning sky, Rebecca and Benjamin exhaustedly looked at the scene in disbelief as tears rolled down their cheeks while smoke rose from the smoldering ash and timbers of their beloved home. Horace huddled close by Benjamin's side as he sadly whimpered. They were still in shock and disbelief that their lives had so tragically and unexpectedly changed in a matter of hours.

As Benjamin left his mother's side and wandered through the ruins of the house, his mind was still trying to process the events from the night before. It was as if he remembered the tragic event through a thick haze. Suddenly, a flicker of light caught his eye as the sun reflected of an object on the dirty charred ground. As he bent down to look closely at what caused the reflection, he noticed three metal buttons still attached to a piece of torn charred fabric resting on the ash covered floor. As Benjamin picked up the blackened piece of fabric, he realized it was the sleeve of a man's tailcoat. He held the fabric in his hand and wiped the dirt from the face of the metal objects with his fingers. The fancy and unique engraving in the center of each brass button, immediately caught his attention. His mind suddenly began to race as he concluded that this sleeve could only belong to someone of financial means and not from a gypsy or thief.

As he folded the revealing evidence and placed it in the pocket of his britches, his mind was heavily troubled as he gazed over the ruins and silently wondered who would commit such a heinous act?

GARY ROWE

Atherton County, Virginia

Early June, 1774

GARY ROWE

Chapter 8

The coach entered the iron gates from the main road and continued onto the pathway leading to Atherton Hall. A familiar scent that Sarah remembered so fondly filled the air and overtook her senses. Memories of her childhood visits to Charles Town came rushing back as the soft afternoon breeze carried that wonderful lemony scent throughout the air. Her wandering mind drifted back to the previous decade when she first developed a fondness for the large white beautiful flower that had fascinated her ever since.

As the Eldridge's coach continued to travel toward Atherton Hall, Sarah's excitement quickly grew as she admired the young magnolia trees through the windows of the coach that had been planted on each side of the pathway. As they got closer to the mansion, two mature magnolia trees fully in bloom could be seen on each side of the newly constructed brick home. An imposing two-story Flemish bond brick structure with four huge chimney stacks rising from the center of its roof and two nearly completed two-story dependencies, connected to the main house by one-story brick hyphens, dominated the landscape. A handsome portico supported by two white columns covered the double entrance doors of the central block adding a simple but classical element to the structure. Workers were busy laying the final bricks and painting woodwork in the unfinished dependencies. When the carriage got closer to the nearest wing, plasterers could be seen through the windows perfecting their craft. A well-dressed gentleman was standing on the stoop of the doorway in deep discussion with another man who was holding a large sheet of paper.

Sarah's enjoyment of that wonderful scent was soon interrupted as the sound of a barking dog rushing to greet the carriage brought her thoughts back to the present.

"Horace! Horace! Calm down, boy!," the well-dressed gentleman called after the animal, as the barking noise and the rumbling of the coach interrupted his conversation. "Easy, Horace!," the gentleman continued as he descended the steps of the dependency and approached the halting carriage.

As the coach slowed to a gradual stop, Sarah's wandering mind slowly came back into focus when she noticed the handsome man walking toward the coach. His striking good looks, athletic build and wavy brown hair with golden highlights, that she assumed were from being outdoors in the sun, created a feeling within her that she had never experienced before.

"Good afternoon, Benjamin," Lawrence Eldridge called out from the window of the carriage to greet the man as he got closer.

"Judge Eldridge, it's a pleasure to see you, sir! Good day to you all," Benjamin replied as he immediately recognized the man in the coach with the letter "E" embossed on its door while Horace continued his barking. "Please, forgive Horace. He gets so excited when guests arrive," Benjamin continued as he reached to pet the animal on the top of his head in hopes he would stop barking. "Welcome to Atherton Hall."

"Benjamin, you do remember my wife, Caroline, but I don't believe you have met our daughter, Sarah," Lawrence said.

"It's nice to see you Mrs. Eldridge," Benjamin replied while he nodded his head at Lawrence's wife. "It's a pleasure, Sarah," Benjamin responded as he took notice of the blonde young lady sitting beside her mother.

"I hope you don't mind our taking the liberty to stop by unannounced. We were visiting friends in Atherton Village and our curiosity led to our visit on our return to Williamsburg. We have heard so much talk in the surrounding counties about the rebuilding of the Atherton family home that we decided to take the opportunity to stop by and see it for ourselves," Lawrence explained.

"You know that you always have an open invitation," Benjamin replied. "Please come in. I know mother would be pleased to see all of you," Benjamin continued while stepping aside as Lawrence exited the coach. "I'll have Isaiah help your driver attend to your horses," Benjamin continued as he motioned to his servant who was standing nearby while glancing at the Eldridge's driver. "The house has been a work in progress," he continued. "However, it is coming along nicely. I'm rather proud of how it is turning out."

"It is beautiful!," Caroline said as she glanced at the brick structure while Lawrence held out his hand to assist his wife when she stepped out of the coach.

When Benjamin stepped forward to take Sarah's hand while she exited the coach, he was suddenly taken aback by the beautiful creature he saw when his eyes met hers. Sarah's fair skin and beautiful blonde hair that circled her heart-shaped face struck him like a bolt of lightning. When their eyes locked for a brief moment, and Benjamin gazed into Sarah's beautiful blue eyes, he sensed a certain innocence that added to her appeal.

"Welcome to Atherton Hall," Benjamin said with a warm smile.

"Thank you," Sarah blushed as Benjamin took her hand in his.

As soon as Sarah stepped out of the coach and onto the ground, Horace began to happily wag his tail while he pressed himself against the folds of fabric in her dress and excitedly looked upward at the strange girl with anticipation. Sarah smiled as she gazed downward at the affectionate animal and began to pat him on the top of his head while Horace continued to wag his tail.

"Oh, how sweet!," Sarah affectionately said as she warmed to the animal.

"It seems Horace has found a new friend," Benjamin admiringly said as he looked at Sarah.

Once everyone was standing on the gravel beside the carriage, Benjamin led the way to the front portico.

"I know both your father John and General Atherton would be so proud of what you have accomplished. They were both great men and they have been missed by many these past couple of years," Lawrence said to congratulate Benjamin and express his sorrow at the same time as they all strolled toward the house.

"Thank you for your kind words, sir," Benjamin replied. "I do miss them so much," he added.

"It is still very difficult to believe they are no longer with us. Your father was a great friend and colleague," Lawrence fondly remembered.

"We always enjoyed your parents visits to our home when they came to Williamsburg," Caroline affectionately said.

"And, of course, I also have fond memories of your grandfather. When I was a young man, just out of law school, I remember when your grandfather came to Williamsburg to petition the Virginia General Assembly to sell lots for his newly founded Atherton Village," Lawrence continued. "I remember him as a kind gentleman," he added while they approached the portico steps.

"Thank you again for all your kind words," Benjamin replied while their fond memories brought painful reminders of the grief he felt over the loss of both men. "Please, come in," he continued in an attempt to shift the conversation while motioning with his hand for them to climb the brick steps.

"Thank you," Caroline said while she paused to reply to Benjamin's invitation. "Your home is lovely. It resembles some of the architecture near our home in Williamsburg," Caroline continued while she glanced at the house once again.

"Williamsburg is a charming town," Benjamin responded while they lingered at the base of the steps.

"And your magnolias smell heavenly! Sarah loves magnolias. They are her favorite flower!," Caroline continued while she looked upward at the two tall mature magnolia trees that towered towards the sky on each side of the house.

"What a coincidence, it is my favorite flower too!," Benjamin smiled at Caroline before turning to notice the expression of delight on Sarah's face.

"That is a coincidence!," Caroline exclaimed.

"When you do anticipate you will have the house completed?," Lawrence asked Benjamin.

"Hopefully, in a few weeks it will be all done," Benjamin answered. "I just wish grandfather could have lived to see it rebuilt," he continued.

"There is no doubt he would be so proud of you," Caroline said.

"Well, I'm sure that your mother is very happy," Lawrence added.

"Yes, she is delighted and has assured me that she knows grandfather would be very proud," Benjamin happily said. "Mother and I are planning on hosting a gathering next month with our family and a few close friends to celebrate the completion of Atherton Hall. Once we finalize our plans, we hope that you will be able to join us," Benjamin continued.

"That would be delightful!," Caroline replied as she excitedly glanced at Lawrence. "Thank you for including us!," she added.

As Benjamin once again motioned with his hand to welcome his guests into his home, he politely stepped aside to allow them to ascend the steps. As Sarah moved gracefully forward, Benjamin took the opportunity to continue to admire the beautiful girl that had taken him by surprise. Her stylish feathered hat and elegant blue gown accentuated her slim figure and a warm feeling overcame him as the two exchanged smiles. As Sarah began to climb the steps, Horace cheerfully followed behind. Once Benjamin joined his guests under the portico, he entered through the entrance doors to usher his guests into the main hall while Horace rushed to join him.

"Please, come in. Mother will be delighted that we have guests," Benjamin invitingly said.

As Sarah and her parents stepped across the threshold, they were unprepared for the beautiful architecture that awaited them inside the house. A spacious entrance hall with high ceilings, decorative wainscoting and beautiful crown molding immediately caught their attention. To the right of the entrance doors was a wide staircase that led to the second floor. The width and scale of the staircase and the decorative woodwork along the edge of the steps made such an impressive statement in the entrance hall.

"Benjamin, is that you? What has caused Horace to go into such a stir? Has he found another squirrel to chase?," Rebecca asked as she appeared from the back of the entrance hall and interrupted everyone's admiration of the impressive room.

"Mother, look who has surprised us with a visit," Benjamin said as she approached, immediately realizing her son was not alone in the hall.

"Caroline and Lawrence! What a wonderful surprise!," Rebecca exclaimed. "Pardon me for not realizing you were here," Rebecca continued as she excitedly hugged her dear friends.

"Please, pardon us," Caroline said. "We are the ones who must apologize for visiting your home unannounced," she continued.

"Please, don't apologize!," Rebecca protested. "It is so good to have you here!," Rebecca fondly added.

"Mother, this is Lawrence and Caroline's daughter, Sarah," Benjamin said to make the introduction.

"Oh, my! You have grown into such a beautiful young lady! I haven't seen you since you were a young girl," Rebecca exclaimed.

"The pleasure is all mine, Mrs. Thompson," Sarah replied. "Atherton Hall is quite lovely," she added.

"Thank you, my dear," Rebecca warmly replied.

"I was telling Benjamin when we arrived how proud John and General Atherton would be of him," Lawrence said to Rebecca.

"Thank you, Lawrence. We do miss them so much," Rebecca replied. "They were both good men and did so much for the Colony of Virginia," she continued.

"That they did. Their contributions will be long remembered and the Atherton legacy will live on," Lawrence sincerely said. "I miss my dear friend, John," he added.

"Your father is to be commended as well. Nathaniel has created a successful empire in the central part of the colony and I know you are so proud of him. I always remember father speaking so highly of your grandfather, Jeremiah, when he reminisced about their army days in England," Rebecca fondly said.

"Thank you. That is so kind of you," Lawrence replied as he and Rebecca shared a warm smile.

"Please, everyone come into the parlor and I'll order us all some refreshment," Rebecca offered as she led everyone into the room to the right of the staircase and pulled the bell rope on the wall to summon a servant.

As the guests entered the parlor, they were immediately captivated by the impressive architectural details and how they equally matched the beauty of the entrance hall. Decorative wainscoting and crown molding surrounded the walls and a handsome fireplace was the main focal point of the imposing room. A beautiful mantle, above the Italian marble casing of the firebox, and decorative wood molding enhanced the fireplace surround. An inviting shade of green graced the plaster walls above the wainscoting.

"Oh, what a beautiful room!," Caroline exclaimed.

"It did turn out rather nicely," Rebecca responded. "I am very well pleased. Although, I do have a few more furniture pieces on order from England."

"What you do have is lovely," Caroline replied as she admired a Chippendale sofa covered in a rich gold damask fabric and a pair of complementary wing chairs.

"What a charming hat you are wearing," Rebecca said to Caroline.

"Why, thank you! As you know, I do have a fondness for them!," Caroline jokingly replied. "I purchased it at a quaint new millinery shop in Williamsburg. The proprietor, Emma, is new to Williamsburg and she and I have become quite friendly. The next time you come to town, we'll have to visit her shop and I'll introduce you to the dear girl," Caroline continued with excitement.

"I would like that," Rebecca responded. "The hat is lovely!," she continued.

"I think Emma looks at me as a maternal figure since she's only a few years older than Sarah," Caroline responded. "For some reason, she seems eager to become friends," she added.

"I will look forward to meeting her," Rebecca replied. "Please be seated and make yourselves comfortable," Rebecca said as she turned her attention to everyone just as a young servant girl appeared in the doorway to answer her mistress's call. "Tula, would you please bring cider and treats for our guests," Rebecca instructed.

"Yes, ma'am," Tula replied as she bowed forward from the doorway and then backed out of the room.

"I do miss a good cup of tea," Rebecca said while they all began to sit down.

"So do I!," Caroline replied.

"It certainly has become the 'forbidden herb' since the Tea Act," Lawrence said in reference to the imposed taxes the legislation caused and was prompted by the destruction of tea in the Boston Harbor the previous year.

After Rebecca and Caroline sat down on the sofa, Sarah took a nearby Queen Anne side chair. Benjamin and Lawrence claimed the two wing chairs while Horace quietly laid down on the floor near Sarah.

"How are things in Williamsburg, Judge Eldridge?," Benjamin asked Lawrence in an effort to restart the conversation.

"Things are quite unsettled. Since Lord Dunmore dissolved the House of Burgesses at the end of March, it has caused the burgesses to reassemble on their own," Lawrence replied.

"I have heard they are issuing calls for the assembly of delegates to be elected for the purpose of establishing constitutions of fundamental law for Virginia," Benjamin said.

"Yes, they want to create a set of fair and just laws for the colonies that are different from British law. Most American colonists are resentful of taxation without representation. Tensions are building and there will undoubtedly be unwelcome consequences for the British government," Lawrence responded.

"I am so thankful that grandfather paid off all his debts to London creditors three years ago. When the London banks failed in '72, they pressured a lot of Virginia planters to settle their accounts which put them in dire financial straits. Thankfully, I did not have to deal with that situation," Benjamin explained.

"Thankfully, my father has fared well also. But is has been different for a lot of Virginia planters since they mostly trade on credit. They are in debt to British merchants and those merchants are demanding to be paid," Lawrence said.

"Since the Scottish and Dutch have opened warehouses and merchant services in the colony, it has helped the smaller planters. They can sell their crop in Virginia and purchase farm tools and other items from those same merchants. Then it eliminates the risk of shipment and sale of their tobacco overseas," Benjamin said on a more positive note. "However, all this political turmoil and resentment is not helping relations between Britain and the colonies," Benjamin continued.

"I agree. I feel the colonies may be on the road to a revolution," Lawrence commented.

While Lawrence and Benjamin continued their discussion on politics and trade, the three women were discussing the current fashion and Caroline was informing Rebecca about the latest Williamsburg social events.

"Thank you, Tula. Please set the tray down over there and I'll serve," Rebecca said while she motioned to the servant girl as she reappeared in the doorway carrying a large tray containing a pitcher of cider and cakes.

After Tula followed her mistress's instructions, she left the room while Rebecca arose to serve her guests.

"You and your mother will have to visit us the next time you come to Williamsburg," Caroline suggested as she glanced at Benjamin and then Rebecca.

"Thank you, how kind. I believe Benjamin is planning a business trip next week," Rebecca said as she smiled at her son, knowing he was taken with the Eldridge's beautiful daughter. "Unfortunately, I won't be joining him this time," she added while she handed her guests a glass of cider and offered them cakes that rested neatly on a decorative porcelain plate.

"Yes. I am attending the meeting of the colony's chief merchants next week," Benjamin said as he and Sarah exchanged smiles.

"Oh, you must dine with us while you are in town!," Caroline offered as she took a bite of the delicious cake.

"Yes, please," Lawrence added while lowering his glass after taking a sip of cider.

"Actually, we have already planned a small supper party," Caroline said.

"Thank you. It would be my pleasure to join you," Benjamin said while hoping he would get to see Sarah again.

"I have invited James Prescott and his wife Clarissa as well as my friend Emma and her escort," Caroline explained. "She hasn't told me who she is bringing," she added.

"I'll look forward to it," Benjamin replied.

"We are sorry you won't be able to join us, Rebecca," Caroline said.

"It sounds like it will be a lovely evening. But I'll definitely look forward to meeting your friend Emma the next time I visit," Rebecca responded.

"That will be nice! And you will definitely love her shop!," Caroline exclaimed.

"Dear, I think it's time we should be continuing on our journey," Lawrence suggested. "We do want to make it to the inn before nightfall," he continued.

"Yes, we have imposed on your hospitality far too long," Caroline apologetically said to her hosts.

"Nonsense," Rebecca said. "It was a pleasure to see you all. We do hope you will visit us again soon."

"Mother, I extended our invitation to Judge and Mrs. Eldridge and Sarah for our upcoming celebration," Benjamin said.

"Yes, we would love for you to join us! Once we finalize the date, we will send you an invitation!," Rebecca happily said.

"We will look forward to it," Lawrence replied as he looked at his wife's smiling face.

"Please let me show you around the grounds before you leave," Benjamin suggested while desiring to remain in Sarah's presence for as long as possible.

"That would be lovely! I know Sarah would enjoy getting a closer look at your magnolia trees," Caroline said.

After Rebecca expressed her sad farewell in the front entrance hall, Benjamin led Sarah and her parents toward the front door to begin their tour of the grounds. When Benjamin reached for the doorknob, Horace darted through the crack in the door and quickly ran down the steps. As Sarah and Benjamin caught up with Horace on the front lawn, the happy canine briskly walked along side of Benjamin as he wagged his tail. When Horace noticed a group of ducks floating in the river near the bank, he eagerly darted ahead of them as he raced to the edge of the river.

"Horace! Calm down, boy!" Benjamin called in an effort to quiet him down. "Horace loves to be outdoors," he added as he turned to look at Sarah.

"It is so beautiful here. I have no doubt you feel fortunate to be able to enjoy the tranquility and peacefulness of your surroundings," Sarah said.

"Honestly, it's sometimes easy to take it all for granted. It's an honor for someone as lovely as you to remind me of my fortunate circumstances," Benjamin replied as they strolled toward one of the mature magnolia trees beside the house while Caroline and Lawrence discreetly walked a few yards behind them.

"God created such beauty in nature. The flowers, trees, sky, the river, the birds...everything seems in perfect complement," Sarah continued as she admired the beauty of her surroundings.

"I feel the same way. Everything is in perfect unison," Benjamin assessed while he appreciated the wisdom of this lovely young lady.

"It's nice to meet someone who appreciates the beauty of nature as much as I do," Sarah said as she smiled at Benjamin. "Your magnolia trees are lovely," she added.

"Thank you. The two larger ones, on each side of the house, have been here for years. They survived the fire because the bark of a magnolia tree will not burn. I'm sure you noticed the newer ones I have planted along the pathway that leads to the house," Benjamin prompted.

"Yes, I admired them as soon as we entered the entrance gates," Sarah replied.

"I rooted the new saplings from the two older trees. It is an interesting process," Benjamin proudly said.

"Really? How is that done?," Sarah enthusiastically inquired.

"I staked the lower limbs into the ground and they eventually took root. Then I dug up the new trees and replanted them," Benjamin explained.

"Oh, how interesting!" Sarah exclaimed.

"Did you know the magnolia tree is native to the southern colonies?," Benjamin asked as a look of interest appeared on Sarah's face. "The species came about centuries ago and were pollinated by beetles before bees were in existence," he informed.

"I have been fascinated with magnolias since I was a child. I regularly visited my aunt and uncle in Charles Town with my parents during early summers. We are retuning later this month for my cousin Lucinda's wedding. Their plantation has numerous magnolia trees and the scent is so exhilarating when it fills the air," she explained.

"Yes, I agree. The scent is quite amazing," Benjamin said.

"I'm sure you've noticed there are a few magnolias in Williamsburg. However, nowhere near as many as in South Carolina," Sarah informed.

"Well, I hope my new plantings are adding to those numbers so we can catch up with South Carolina," Benjamin teased.

"I will not complain with your endeavor!," Sarah said as she laughed at his playfulness.

"This has turned out to be such a delightful day," Benjamin replied.

"Yes, it has been a joy to see your lovely home," Sarah responded as she and Benjamin paused beneath the magnolia tree.

"Let me present you with a magnolia blossom to take with you," Benjamin said as he reached to a low hanging limb to retrieve a blossom in full bloom.

"Oh, how lovely!," Sarah said as she blushed when Benjamin presented her with the fragrant white flower.

While Benjamin watched Sarah admiring the beautiful flower she had loved since childhood, he knew he would remember this moment forever while being captivated by her innocence and beauty.

"I'm disappointed we haven't had the opportunity to meet before now," Benjamin said as they turned to stroll towards the house. "I guess it's understandable since I have been away for a while in England at school," he continued.

"And I have been back and forth between Williamsburg and Penderley to care for my grandmother Eldridge during her long illness," Sarah said. "That would explain why our paths have never crossed," she added.

"How unfortunate for us both," Benjamin replied.

"We have so much enjoyed our visit. Atherton Hall is lovely and we appreciate your generous hospitality," Caroline said to Benjamin as she and Lawrence joined them from behind.

"It has been my pleasure," Benjamin replied.

"And please thank your mother again for her hospitality," Caroline said.

"We will look forward to seeing you next week in Williamsburg," Lawrence said as they walked toward the coach.

"It will be my honor to be your guest," Benjamin replied as Lawrence helped Caroline board the coach.

"Thank you for the lovely magnolia," Sarah said as she smiled at Benjamin and raised the flower to her face to smell the lemony fragrance.

While Benjamin returned her smile and raised his hand to assist her into the coach, Horace began to press himself against Sarah's dress once again and wag his tail.

"It was a pleasure to meet you Horace," Sarah said as she reached down to warmly pet the animal that was obviously taken with her.

"We will see you next week," Lawrence said to Benjamin as the driver signaled the horses to move ahead.

"I hope you all have a safe journey on your return home," Benjamin called out as the coach began to advance down the long pathway toward the entrance gates.

While Horace sat closely beside Benjamin and continued to wag his tail, Benjamin said, "I know you like her, boy! I do too!," as a warm feeling overcame him while he thought about the lovely girl that had suddenly come into his life.

As Benjamin watched the coach disappear from his view, he knew that his thoughts would constantly be of Sarah until he had the opportunity to see her once again.

Williamsburg, Virginia

Mid-June, 1774

GARY ROWE

Chapter 9

Benjamin rode his horse into the east end of Williamsburg and onto York Street while his thoughts were constantly of Sarah. The vision of her beautiful face and her sweet nature, that he first experienced during their recent introduction at Atherton Hall, would not leave his thoughts. The Eldridge's invitation to dine at Hemsworth House during his stay in Williamsburg was a welcome one, since it would place him in the presence of Sarah once again.

While Benjamin continued through the east end of town, his appearance created an impressive image to bystanders as he sat proudly in his English saddle. His horse Thunder, a fine black thoroughbred who was sixteen hands high, safely brought him to the end of his journey. His first stop, at Christiana Campbell's Tavern – being a short block further on Waller Street – would secure him a resting place during his stay.

From an early age, Benjamin knew the tavern had the reputation of being one of the most prominent taverns in the capital. His father, John, frequently visited the establishment since his occupation as a lawyer regularly took him to the capital for business. As Benjamin grew older, John would sometimes bring along his wife and son. When the General Assembly was in session, Campbell's tavern was one of the principal places where members of the House of Burgesses lodged. John made it clear to his family that he preferred his stay even more during less hectic times. Christiana Campbell advertised her tavern as providing "genteel accommodations and the very best entertainment" and Benjamin and his family knew from those experiences that her claims proved to be true. The tavern was famous for providing rooms and food for those who had business to conduct with government officials or in the General Court and those who attended the regular meetings of the colony's chief merchants. Since these meetings brought many attendees to the town, the taverns and lodges would fill up quickly and Christiana Campbell's Tavern was always a popular place to lodge.

Mrs. Campbell's white clapboard tavern was known for its spaciousness. The steeply sloping gambrel roof with six pedimented windows created an even more sense of roominess on the second floor. The exterior of the tavern was one-and-one half stories high and the roof line that scooped over the long porches extended entirely across the front and gave the building a low rambling appearance. The narrow structure rested on unusually high foundation walls and large brick chimneys with T-shaped stacks accented both ends of the building. The front porch was embellished with wood railings and square posts and a flight of limestone steps led to the double entrance doors in the center of the porch.

Once Benjamin arrived at Christiana's tavern, he lowered himself to the ground and led his beloved horse to the trough for a drink of water. After handing Thunder's reins to a waiting stable boy and tipping him with a shiny coin from his pocket, Benjamin made his way up the steps and into the establishment. As soon as he entered through the doorway, the proprietor herself entered from an adjoining door into the hall.

"Mr. Thompson! It's a pleasure to see you! I'm sure you are in town for the gathering of merchants," Christiana assumed as she immediately recognized her familiar lodger.

"Yes, and it will give me the opportunity to take care of some business matters. This is going to be a good year for my tobacco crop. I was hoping you could provide me with accommodations for a couple of days," Benjamin said.

"The meeting is bringing quite a few lodgers. But, of course, you know I always have a place for you, Mr. Thompson," Christiana happily replied.

After checking in at the front desk and settling in his room upstairs, he decided to take a quick nap to recover from his journey. Benjamin later awakened refreshed and eager to join the Eldridge's for supper. As he opened his eyes from his short rest, thoughts of Sarah immediately came to his mind. Her beautiful heart-shaped face and kind nature had captivated him like no one else before and the contemplation of seeing her again constantly consumed his thoughts.

When he began changing his clothes in preparation for his evening plans, he dressed in a simple but stylish beige tailcoat and britches. After tying his hair into a pony tail and making a final stop at the looking glass that hung on the wall to assess his appearance, he rejoined Thunder outside.

Benjamin guided Thunder onto Duke of Gloucester Street and continued toward the west end of town. After entering the west side of Palace Street and passing Bruton Parish Church, the Eldridge's house came into view. As he approached the Georgian house that faced the Palace Green, he immediately thought of Caroline's comparison of Atherton Hall and its similarity to the architecture of Williamsburg. Even though he was familiar with the house and well aware of the its reputation as one of the handsomest houses in the town, it seemed to draw his interest more than ever before due to his recent introduction to one particular resident that constantly entertained his thoughts.

The impressive façade of Hemsworth House, although more modest than Atherton Hall, was constructed of red brick with white woodwork and the structure was perfectly symmetrical. The entrance was reached by a small flight of brick steps with a large door having raised panels and a transom window. The first floor had two windows on each side of the center entrance door and the five windows of the second floor were in perfect alignment with the windows below. The hip roof had two brick chimneys rising from the side slopes of the roof. The roof was supported by a modillion cornice at the top of its brick walls. The lighter-colored bricks, framing the windows and doors, were laid with "rubbed bricks." Benjamin especially admired this architectural effect that was created when the masons would rub one side of the bricks against each other until a rosy color became evident. For a moment, he wished he had incorporated that design in the building of Atherton Hall. However, he quickly dismissed the thought since he was proud of the architectural elements he had chosen for his home. In his final assessment of Hemsworth House, he admired the beveled water table at the base of the structure and the walls, similar to Atherton Hall, that were laid in a Flemish bond pattern.

As Benjamin brought Thunder to a halt and lowered himself onto the edge of the street in front of the house, he gave his beloved animal a pat on the neck before tying him to the hitching post.

"Good boy, Thunder! Good boy," Benjamin affectionately said as he loosened the saddle cinch and then pulled an apple from his saddlebag to give it to Thunder as a treat.

Thunder happily whinnied when his master presented him with the firm round red fruit causing Benjamin to affectionately give his prized horse another pat on the neck.

After climbing the brick steps and firmly knocking on the wood paneled front door, a dark-skinned girl wearing a white cap over her black hair politely greeted him as she opened the door. A long white apron was tied at her waist and covered the front of her cotton floral print dress.

"I am Benjamin Thompson. I believe the Eldridges are expecting me," Benjamin said.

"Yes, sir. Right this way," she replied as she stepped aside for him to enter.

When Benjamin entered the entrance hallway, he vaguely remembered the simple but elegant architectural elements that graced the interior due to his occasional visits as a child. The walls were white-washed with crown molding and chair rail that were painted in steel blue and black baseboards met wide planked pine floors. A staircase rose on the left side of the passageway and the wide entrance hall contained four doors leading to each room on the first floor. Benjamin heard several voices coming from the parlor located on the left side of the hall. As he glanced into the dining room to the right of the hall, he noticed two servants attending to the table in preparation for the upcoming meal. A bowfat could be seen in the corner of the room beside the fireplace and wainscoting adorned the walls.

After the servant girl motioned with her hand toward the parlor and presented Benjamin to his hosts and their other guests, she politely bowed and disappeared back into the hallway. Caroline and Lawrence immediately arose and greeted Benjamin in the doorway of the parlor. Lawrence represented the perfect southern gentleman dressed in an embroidered gray silk tailcoat and Caroline was equally impressive wearing a soft blue gown accented with a ruffled white bodice and matching petticoat. Her brown hair was elegantly styled and decorated with a strand of white pearls.

"Welcome, Benjamin! Please come in," Lawrence smilingly said. "Sarah will be down shortly. We are so glad to have her back home after her extended stay at Penderley," he added, sensing Benjamin's infatuation with his daughter.

"Benjamin, you know James Prescott but I don't believe you have met his wife, Clarissa," Caroline said as James arose from chair. "They will be joining us for dinner. And may I introduce Benjamin Thompson," she continued as she looked at Clarissa and then back at Benjamin.

"It is a pleasure to meet you," Benjamin said as he nodded his head at Clarissa and reached to shake James's hand.

"The pleasure is all mine," Clarissa said as she returned the nicety. "Are you Mr. Thompson of Atherton County?," Clarissa inquisitively asked.

"Yes, I am. My grandfather founded Atherton Village," Benjamin proudly answered. "Are you acquainted with my family?," Benjamin asked while Caroline motioned for him to take a seat.

"No," Clarissa replied. "It's just that your family is very well-known and it is an honor to meet you. I have heard James and his mother Naomi speak highly of your family many times," she continued.

"Thank you," Benjamin responded while they all sat down.

While everyone continued to engage in light conversation, Benjamin silently thought how surprised he was when Clarissa was introduced as James's wife. His first impression was that they couldn't possibly be husband and wife since it was obvious there were a number of years in age between the couple. Benjamin could easily understand what James would see in Clarissa, obviously being in her early twenties, but not sure what Clarissa would see in him. Clarissa's dark brown hair, fair skin and alluring figure was enough to make any man stop and take notice. Her dark hair, piled high on her head, created an elegant appearance and was further enhanced with coiled ringlets that fell in the back at the nape of her neck. She wore a stylish emerald green gown that complemented her desirable figure and her low-cut décolletage accentuated her full round breasts. The diamonds in her necklace and earrings sparkled as the precious stones reflected the light from the candles that illuminated the room. Clarissa gave an initial impression of a well-bred lady but Benjamin's instincts told him that she was not what she appeared to be. James, on the other hand, was a plain and quiet well-mannered gentleman with a little fullness around his waistline. His fashionable dark blue tailcoat and britches, along with his white silk stockings and perfectly powdered wig represented aristocracy at its best. Other than their obvious impeccable taste in clothing, the couple seemed an unlikely pair due to their obvious difference in attractiveness. Benjamin was well aware of the Prescott's reputation in society and their status as a well-to-do Virginia planter family who lived on the James River south of Williamsburg due to his mother and James's mother's friendship.

While Benjamin was pondering over his thoughts, a knock at the front door interrupted everyone's conversation.

"Our final guests must have arrived!," Caroline excitedly announced.

"Good evening!," Caroline said with surprise to her last set of guests as the young female servant ushered them into the parlor from the entrance hall. "Let me introduce Emma Adams. Emma is relatively new to Williamsburg but we have become quite friendly in a short amount of time!," Caroline continued while still in shock of Emma's choice of escort. "And, of course, everyone knows Alexander Drake," Caroline said while trying to hide her animosity toward Alexander as she and Lawrence traded a meaningful and confused look.

Clarissa and James immediately exchanged greetings with the couple before Emma focused her attention on Benjamin.

"Hello, I'm Emma Adams," Emma said to introduce herself to Benjamin.

"It's a pleasure to meet you, Emma," Benjamin warmly replied. "Are you any relation to the Adams's of Atherton Village?," he asked.

"Possibly. My late husband did have a lot of relatives in Virginia. It is a rather common name, isn't it?," she added while Benjamin politely smiled.

"Alexander and I are acquainted," Benjamin said with a puzzled look as he wondered why this man was in Judge Eldridge's home and reluctantly shook his hand out of politeness.

Benjamin knew of Alexander's shady reputation and opposition to his father John in the courtroom. Benjamin would never forget a particular trial that occurred almost a decade earlier. His father John had been the prosecuting lawyer for the famous treason trial involving a man named Simon Bartram and Alexander had been the defense lawyer. John always doubted Alexander's ethics as a lawyer and his deceptive defense tactics of trying to win a case even when Alexander knew his client was guilty. John had always expressed distrust of Alexander and Benjamin knew that Lawrence shared the same opinion and wondered why this man was a guest in Lawrence's home.

However, Benjamin guessed by Caroline and Lawrence's reaction that they had no idea who Emma had invited as her escort. He also assumed that Lawrence had to maintain a civil relationship with Alexander due to their association in the court system. Although, Benjamin felt sorry for Emma believing that she couldn't possibly know the true Alexander or she would not be involved with someone who was so unscrupulous. Also, by knowing his hosts' good manners, Benjamin felt that Lawrence and Caroline would tolerate Alexander for the sake of their friendship with Emma.

Ironically, Benjamin's assessment of Alexander and Emma was completely opposite of that of James and Clarissa. Although Emma appeared to be around the same age as Clarissa, and Alexander a few years older, they were more believable as a suited match especially since Alexander appeared younger than his actual age. Emma was an attractive woman with an alluring figure and her appearance was similar to Clarissa but she portrayed herself in a way that was almost purposely down played. The plain appearance that she presented seemed contrived. Her fair skin was flawless and her dark brown hair was plainly styled in an understated lady-like fashion. She wore a soft champagne colored gown that was elegant but less revealing and more modestly designed. On the other hand, Benjamin knew

Alexander was considered attractive by most women due to his handsome looks, fashionable dress and charming persona. Even with those contrasts in their appearance, Emma and Alexander would easily be accepted as a couple. Although, Benjamin knew that Alexander was not a man of moral character.

While Benjamin was mulling over his inner thoughts, a delightful vision suddenly appeared in the doorway of the parlor.

"Good evening, everyone," Sarah said as she entered from the entrance hall.

"Hello, dear!," Caroline said to her daughter. "Don't you look lovely!," she quickly added.

Benjamin suddenly felt a warm feeling overcome him as his eyes rested on the beautiful girl that had unexpectedly taken him by surprise upon their first meeting the week before. Her lovely blonde hair, fashionably styled, and her perfectly fitted pink silk gown adorned with rows of white lace cascading from the edge of the sleeves presented a lovely portrait of innocence and charm.

Sarah's face lit up when she saw the handsome young man as she entered the room. When their eyes met, it was as if they could read each other's thoughts. They both had been anticipating the time they would see each other again. Sarah was anxious to know more about this man that had brought new meaning to her life and was hoping this evening would allow her the opportunity to do just that.

She had heard that Benjamin was an extremely discerning man for his young age of twenty-four. He was known for having a quick mind and was very shrewd when dealing with business matters. It was common knowledge in the surrounding counties that Benjamin took great pride and responsibility with what he had inherited and was determined to preserve his family's legacy. She knew that to be true after having the opportunity to visit Atherton Hall and witnessing what he had accomplished. Sarah admired his determination and was naturally taken with his handsome looks, thick brown hair and piercing blue eyes that were enough to make any woman swoon. She also admired his ability to look effortlessly neat and elegant in less formal clothing, as he did during their first meeting, and even more so this evening dressed in formal good taste. Sarah thought his confident attitude only added to his attractiveness.

"Good evening, Sarah," Benjamin said as he walked toward her.

"It is nice to see you again, Benjamin," Sarah replied as she held out her hand. "Welcome to our home."

"Thank you for your hospitality," Benjamin replied as he took her hand in his. "It is a pleasure to see you again as well," he added while continuing to hold her hand.

While Benjamin and Sarah stood gazing into each other's eyes, they barely noticed the young servant girl arrive to inform Caroline that supper was ready to be served.

"Let's all move to the dining room," Caroline suggested as she and Lawrence led the way across the hall.

Once everyone had entered the dining room, Caroline began seating her guests.

"I thought it would be a good idea if each couple sat across from one another," Caroline said as the couples heeded to her suggestion. "That will allow us to get to know one another a little better," she continued while moving toward her Queen Anne armchair at one end of the table. "Benjamin, you and Sarah can sit across from one another next to Lawrence," she motioned with her hand while Lawrence moved to his chair at the head of the table.

"Oh, what beautiful flowers!," Emma said as she admired the arrangement that had been placed in a crystal bowl in the center of the beautifully appointed table while everyone claimed their seats.

"The roses came from my garden," Caroline proudly said as two manservants entered the room.

"Yes, they are mother's pride and joy," Sarah affectionately added as she smiled at her mother.

"Let me make a toast," Lawrence said while the two manservants were moving around the table and filling each crystal glass with wine. "To everyone's health and prosperity!," he pronounced while raising his glass as the two servants left the room.

"To health and prosperity!," everyone exclaimed as they cheerfully raised their glasses and echoed Lawrence's salute.

"And much success to this session of the Meeting of Merchants!," Lawrence added after taking a sip from his glass and placing it back down on the table.

"I agree. Hopefully, these gatherings will continue to create good relations between merchants and planters for the benefit of our economy," Benjamin said.

"Yes, especially with tensions building between the colonies and Great Britain," James added.

"I hear that you have a successful plantation south of Williamsburg," Clarissa interrupted as she turned her head toward her right to look at Benjamin sitting beside her. "Word has traveled throughout the counties of your impressive home," she added.

"Benjamin's home is beautiful!," Caroline exclaimed as the two manservants returned with a platter of roasted pork and bowls of potatoes and seasonal vegetables.

"And his magnolia trees are lovely!," Sarah said as she warmly smiled at Benjamin who was sitting directly across from her while the manservants began serving.

"I understand that you have recently rebuilt your home," Emma said as she looked at Benjamin to her far left on the other side of the table.

"Sadly, our family home burned on Christmas morning two-and-a-half years ago," Benjamin answered as he noticed Emma glance at Alexander who sat directly across from her.

"Oh, I am so sorry to hear," Emma said to break the temporary moment of silence. "May I be so bold to ask what happened?," she inquired.

"It's unclear what caused the misfortune. Tragically, my father and grandfather died in the fire," Benjamin replied. "It's been difficult, especially for mother," Benjamin added as he looked to his left at Alexander while Alexander reached for his wine glass and raised it to take sip.

"Oh, how awful!," Emma replied as she quickly glanced back at Benjamin with a look of sympathy.

"Yes, I was sorry to hear of John's death...And your grandfather also," Alexander quickly added while Benjamin was shocked and taken aback as he noticed the fancy buttons along Alexander's sleeve.

Benjamin's normally warm blue eyes suddenly turned cold while Sarah immediately noticed Benjamin's change in mood.

"The colony lost two great men," Lawrence kindly said while he noticed a strange expression suddenly appear on Benjamin's face.

"Thank you, Judge Eldridge," Benjamin replied in appreciation while regaining control of his emotions. "Emma, I understand that you are relatively new to Williamsburg," Benjamin said to change the subject as he looked back at her to his far left across the table.

"Yes, I am new in town. Although, I have been living on the outskirts of Williamsburg for a number of years," Emma responded.

"What brought you to this charming town?," Benjamin asked.

"I am originally from the northern part of the colony and moved south when I married," Emma explained. "My husband, Patrick, died from a tragic fall three years ago and I finally came to realize I needed a change in my life," Emma answered.

"Please accept my condolences," Benjamin replied.

"Thank you. Yes, it was a tragedy. Although, I have always wanted to own a millinery shop and thought that Williamsburg would be an ideal place to do so. I even worked in one when I was a young girl," Emma answered. "The financial means I was bequeathed upon my husband's death has allowed me to live comfortably and fulfill my dream," she continued.

"I wish you all the best in your new endeavor," Benjamin said.

"My shop is on the northside of Duke of Gloucester Street at the corner of Botetourt Street," Emma informed. "You'll have to visit while you are in town. I'm sure I have something that your mother would love," she added. "Or possibly a special young lady in your life," she continued with a smile.

"She does have the most adorable things!," Caroline interjected as she glanced at Benjamin and then Sarah.

"Oh, before I forget, your order has arrived," Emma said to Caroline. "The items you ordered are of very fine quality," she added.

"I am excited to see them. I may stop by sometime tomorrow," Caroline said.

"I'll make sure your order is ready first thing in the morning," Emma replied as she lowered her fork.

"Thank you, dear," Caroline responded.

"How are you enjoying your new home?," Lawrence asked Clarissa.

"It's such a showplace and living on the James River makes it special!," Clarissa replied as she glanced at Alexander.

"Yes, father was quite proud of his accomplishment," James replied. "I was fortunate to inherit the rewards of his success," he added. "Although, King George's policies toward the colonies are stifling the hopes of us planters for continued prosperity," he added.

"I don't think that the colonies could survive without the support of Great Britain," Alexander said.

"How can you say that, Alexander?," Lawrence said in frustration. "King George is using the colonies to make Great Britain a richer nation," Lawrence said in rebuttal.

"He certainly is!," Benjamin agreed to confirm Lawrence's sentiment.

"Lawrence, please don't talk about politics, dear," Caroline interjected. "Let's talk about more pleasant things," she added.

"James, I was surprised when you decided to marry after all these years of being a bachelor," Alexander stated with a little sarcasm as he glanced at James and then at Clarissa with raised eyebrows.

"Yes, we were all surprised," Emma echoed Alexander's statement. "Clarissa, I hope you realize how lucky you are to have married a man so generous and kind," Emma continued. "My late husband's family and the Prescotts have known each other for years," she added.

"I'm the lucky one," James happily said. "Clarissa is originally from the northern part of the colony also. I'm surprised that you two haven't crossed paths before," James suggested to Emma as he admiringly glanced at his wife.

"That's not so unimaginable, dear," Clarissa quickly interjected while being annoyed with James for being too forthcoming. "I also moved away at a young age when I married. Unfortunately, I too was widowed before I met James," she said while ingenuously smiling at Emma.

"How did you and James meet?," Emma persisted.

"I met him at a dance at Raleigh Tavern," Clarissa proudly answered. "He saw me standing on the side of the room all alone and timidly approached me," Clarissa remembered while Emma and Alexander gave her a suspicious look.

"And I couldn't believe that someone as beautiful as her, would notice me," James graciously replied as he admired his wife while Emma sympathetically looked at him.

"He was so sweet and kind and the perfect gentleman," Clarissa said as she glanced at everyone and then became surprised and angered when she noticed Alexander rolling his eyes.

"Did you all save room for dessert?," Caroline interjected after dabbing her mouth with her napkin while being confused by the undercurrent of emotions she sensed at the table.

"Our cook makes a delicious pound cake," Sarah said in an attempt to ease the atmosphere as she realized what her mother was sensing.

Caroline continued to steer the conversation toward a lighter mood, including remarks about the weather and the crowds of people and social events that the merchant's meeting brought to town, as the main courses to the meal came to an end. The manservants returned with trays of dried fruit, nuts, small cakes and cheese. The gentlemen enjoyed a glass of port while the ladies enjoyed a sweet wine.

As the dinner drew to a close, Caroline invited the ladies back to the parlor. The men arose out of social politeness while the ladies left the room and then reclaimed their seats around the dining room table to continue drinking and conversing.

While Benjamin sat at the dining room table, the discussion led to politics. Although he would normally have plenty to say on the subject, his mind was preoccupied with thoughts of the familiar buttons he saw along Alexander's sleeve as well as the tense but confusing conversation he observed during dinner. For some odd reason, Benjamin sensed there was a connection between Emma, Clarissa and Alexander.

Later, when Benjamin thanked his hosts at the front door for a lovely evening, his thoughts returned to the young lady of the household that had won his admiration.

"Thank you again for your kind hospitality," Benjamin said to Caroline, Lawrence and Sarah while they all stood in the entrance hall.

"We are so glad you decided to join us," Caroline happily said.

"I'm sure I will see you again while you are in town," Lawrence assumed.

"That is most likely since I have to attend to a few things in court," Benjamin informed.

"Yes, we all hope to see you again," Caroline said to Benjamin before glancing at Sarah.

"I enjoyed our time together," Benjamin replied before he turned to Sarah and looked deeply into her blue eyes. "I hope to see you again soon," he continued.

"I'm sure our paths will cross again," Sarah replied with a smile as she looked dreamily back into his eyes, while Caroline smiled as she witnessed their intimate exchange.

While Benjamin rode Thunder back to the tavern, his thoughts returned to the disturbing information he had learned during the evening and he knew he would not rest until he figured out what it all meant.

GARY ROWE

Chapter 10

The following morning, after a restless night of tossing and turning in bed, Benjamin awoke early in his room at Christiana's tavern. When he opened his eyes, the first thing that entered his thoughts were the events of the previous evening. His shocking suspicions consumed his whole being. Although, the thought of Sarah brought some comfort to his troubled mind.

While he stood shaving his face in front of the looking glass that hung above a shelf on the wall, he thought to himself how glad he was to have a full schedule of business ahead of him to keep his concerned mind occupied during the day. After enjoying a light breakfast and making a quick trip to the stables to check on Thunder, Benjamin made his way on foot to the Capitol.

As Benjamin left the tavern stables and crossed Waller Street on his short walk to the meeting, his mind was still distracted by what he had observed the previous evening. Any hopes of leisure that he had planned to combine with business on this trip, had definitely been interrupted. But fortunately, his common sense quickly reminded him of his purpose for being here and what the planters and merchants hoped to accomplish at this particular meeting.

Benjamin had made plans months ago to attend this important meeting of the colony's chief merchants. He could not believe that June of 1774 had arrived and that it had been nearly two-and-a-half years since his father and grandfather had passed. Benjamin wished that the three of them could have attended this meeting together to represent themselves and the other farmers in the communities of Atherton County.

Williamsburg's Meeting of Merchants was an association which developed to meet the needs of business in a decentralized agricultural economy. One of the most important tasks of the meeting was to determine, through bids and offers, the rate of sterling exchange. The value of local currency, in terms of British sterling, varied considerably and was affected by many factors such as the price level and the volume of imports and exports. Sterling bills of exchange were derived from sales of agricultural products abroad and represented the bulk of the colony's negotiable wealth. These bills of exchange were used to pay for the imports of manufactured goods. Virginians produced goods for exchange and some kind of a system of business was necessary to provide the process for exchange.

Benjamin's main purpose for attending was to ensure that his fellow planters and merchants were fairly represented in this established system of business and were not unfairly taken advantage of by the Crown.

Benjamin had a legacy to protect as well as the financial security of his holdings and assets. While the Governor served as the royal authority in Virginia, the Council, House of Burgesses and the General Court served as representatives of the colony's property owners. It was important for the planters and merchants to have their input and these important political sessions created a pathway for how a republican form of self-government was formed by an essentially feuding governing class.

As Benjamin approached the Capitol, he recalled hearing that this particular meeting of the colony's chief merchants, brought seventy-two merchants to attend who felt it necessary to proclaim, for the future, that they were resolved and determined to meet in Williamsburg every 25th day of October and April. Benjamin agreed that these scheduled meetings would serve as public notice for anyone who had business to transact and would allow them to know when to attend. Since merchants and planters from all parts of the colony would be in Williamsburg together for these meetings, it would give them the opportunity to settle accounts, make payments, and buy and sell bills of exchange on Great Britain.

While Benjamin observed the crowds of people that the meeting had brought to Williamsburg, he realized that these meetings would also allow the merchant and planter, who spent most of the year in a relatively isolated location, to enjoy a time of amusement. It allowed them to take advantage of the opportunity to witness horse races, cock fights and theatre performances. During the day, people hurried back and forth from the taverns to the Capitol on business and the nighttime hours provided a time for carousing and drinking. However, Benjamin much rather preferred the peace and serenity of Atherton Hall and its surrounding natural beauty. As he walked into the Capitol, a feeling of warmth overcame him when he thought of the beautiful girl that shared his love for the beauty of nature.

On the west end of town at Hemsworth House, Sarah awoke later than usual after a somewhat restless night. As she opened her eyes, a smile quickly formed across her face as she thought of Benjamin and the joy she felt when being in his presence. While envisioning his handsome face, she remembered Benjamin's change in mood that occurred halfway through dinner the previous evening. While she lay staring at the ceiling, Sarah wondered if his change in mood had anything to do with the unusual and emotional conversation they experienced at the dinner table. Once she dressed and descended the stairs in the front entrance hall, Sarah noticed her mother sitting in the front parlor as she walked past the doorway.

"Good morning, dear," Caroline greeted her daughter as Sarah looked through the doorway. "Did you sleep well?," Caroline asked while she placed her coffee cup back on its saucer and sat it on the table beside her chair.

"For the most part. Although, I woke up a few times during the night," Sarah replied as she walked into the room.

"Is something bothering you, dear?," Caroline asked while Sarah sat in a nearby chair.

"I am still thinking about that unusual conversation at the dinner table last night," Sarah answered.

"I have been thinking about it too," Caroline replied.

"How much do you know about Emma?," Sarah asked.

"Emma has been eager to become friends in the short time she has been in town, although she hasn't been very forthcoming about her past," Caroline replied.

"I have the feeling that Emma and Clarissa know more about each other than they have been letting on," Sarah said.

"I feel the same way. However, Emma has known James for a while due to her late husband's association with the Prescott family but Clarissa has been very private about her past as well," Caroline responded. "Your father thought the conversation was rather strange also when I mentioned it after everyone had left last night," she added.

"Where is father this morning?," Sarah inquired.

"He left early this morning. He had some business to attend to at the courthouse," Caroline explained.

"Sarah, I was wondering if sometime today you wouldn't mind going to Emma's shop to pick up my order?," Caroline asked. "It's a lovely day. The sun is shining and there is a pleasant breeze blowing," she continued.

"I would enjoy the walk," Sarah said as she glanced through the window from her chair at the morning sunshine filtering through the trees.

"And if you are lucky, maybe you'll be fortunate to see Benjamin," Caroline teased.

"Oh, mother!," Sarah retorted in response to her mother's hopes. "That would be nice but I'm sure he is occupied with business today," Sarah continued as she and her mother shared a smile while hearing a knock on the front door.

"I wonder who that could be? We are not expecting anyone," Caroline said.

"I'll see who it is," Sarah said as she stood to walk toward the front entrance hall.

When Sarah opened the front door, a messenger handed her a note addressed to her mother. After returning to parlor, Sarah handed the note to her mother and watched a surprised look appear on Caroline's face.

"It's a note from Emma," Caroline explained after breaking the seal and unfolding the piece of parchment paper. "It is an expression of thanks," she continued as she began to read the contents out loud.

16, June 1774

Dearest Caroline,

I wanted to take a quick moment to thank you for your recent invitation to dine. Alexander and I thoroughly enjoyed the evening. Delicious food and wonderful conversation made the evening a special delight.

It was nice to meet your very interesting guest, Benjamin Thompson.

Thank you again for your thoughtfulness.

Sincerely,
Emma B. Adams

"That was very thoughtful," Sarah said after her mother had finished reading the note.

"Emma seems to be a very kind and thoughtful person. Although, I am still in disbelief that she asked Alexander to be her escort. If she knew his true character, she would not associate herself with him," Caroline said with astonishment.

"Yes, it does seem rather strange," Sarah said while deep in thought.

"Would you like a cup of coffee?," Caroline asked while interrupting her daughter's wandering mind.

"No thank you, mother," Sarah politely answered. "I think I'll go back upstairs and get ready to take that walk to Emma's shop," Sarah continued as she began to arise from her chair.

"Put on something nice," Caroline teased. "You never know who you may run into," Caroline added with a playful smile as Sarah began to leave the room.

"Oh, mother!," Sarah playfully responded as she disappeared through the doorway of the parlor and began to cheerfully ascend the staircase in the front entrance hall.

A while later, on the east side of town, cheers arose as the merchant's meeting fulfilled its mission. Benjamin filtered through the crowds inside the Capitol building as the Meeting of Merchants disbanded. As he left the steps of the Capitol and walked along the brick walkway toward Duke of Gloucester Street, he suddenly stopped as he heard the sound of a familiar voice calling him from behind.

"Benjamin!," the voice called as Benjamin paused and turned to see a red-headed gentleman approaching him on the walkway.

"Mr. Jefferson," Benjamin replied as the man reached outward to shake his hand.

"How are you?," Thomas Jefferson asked. "I never had the opportunity to properly express my condolences for the death of your father and General Atherton," Thomas sincerely said. "I was saddened when I heard of their passing. They were both honorable men," he continued.

"Thank you," Benjamin replied. "It has been difficult. Especially for mother," he added.

"Please give Mrs. Thompson my sincere sympathy," Thomas kindly said. "I hear you have nearly completed rebuilding the Atherton family home," he continued.

"Yes, I'm rather pleased with how it has turned out," Benjamin proudly responded.

"I hear it is quite impressive," Thomas replied.

"I also have heard about your efforts as well," Benjamin politely said.

"My home is a work in progress. It has gone through quite a few revisions. I can't make up my mind as to the final style," Thomas explained.

"If you ever find yourself in Atherton County, please visit us. Mother would be pleased to see you," Benjamin replied.

"And of course, you know that you also have an open invitation. The next time you visit Charlottesville, Martha and I would be pleased to welcome you into our home," Thomas offered.

After more congenial conversation, including comments about the progress made at the merchant's meeting, politics and discussing their tobacco plants that they both predicted would yield a successful crop in a few months, they parted ways on the walkway. As Benjamin continued out of the gate in the brick wall that surrounded the Capitol building and walked onto Duke of Gloucester Street, his mind refocused on the previous evening. While he strolled along the brick sidewalk on his way to the Courthouse on the west end of town, thoughts of the buttons that he observed on Alexander's sleeve gave him an uneasy feeling. After reaching the Courthouse to conduct his usual business matters, and also taking the opportunity to converse with Lawrence, Benjamin returned to Duke of Gloucester Street to make his way back to the tavern on the east side of town. As he stepped onto the sidewalk from the Courthouse steps, he suddenly recalled Emma's suggestion to purchase a gift for his mother. Benjamin strangely thought that a visit to Emma's shop might somehow provide him with an opportunity to discover some useful clues to his newfound suspicions.

A short time before Benjamin began his walk to the tavern, Sarah left Hemsworth House. After crossing the

Palace Green, she continued down Duke of Gloucester Street towards Emma's shop. While she happily strolled along the brick sidewalk enjoying the warmth of the sun and the pleasant light breeze, and occasionally speaking to friendly and familiar faces as they passed by, thoughts of Benjamin joyfully entertained her mind. As she approached Emma's shop at the corner of Duke of Gloucester and Botetourt Streets, she accidentally dropped her handkerchief on the sidewalk a few feet from the corner of the building where the two streets intersected. After bending over to pick up her handkerchief and while attempting to regain her composure, she heard two familiar voices on the sidewalk around the corner.

"Do you think anyone was suspicious of us last night?," the female voice anxiously asked while Sarah stood perfectly still to listen.

"Don't worry, no one suspects a thing," the male voice replied.

"We may have to use Sarah and Benjamin in our plan," the female voice continued.

"Yes, they could be very useful," the male voice responded while Sarah began to take a step forward to look around the corner of the building to see who was talking.

"Sarah!," a familiar voice called her from behind, causing her to suddenly stop while interrupting her attempt to continue to eavesdrop.

"Oh!," Sarah replied while slightly jumping after being startled. "Hello!," Sarah continued after turning to see Benjamin walking toward her on the sidewalk.

"It's nice to see you again," Benjamin happily said as he approached her. "I was just on my way back to the tavern after a quick stop at the Courthouse. I saw your father while I was there," he continued.

"It's nice to see you also. I was just on my way to Emma's shop to pick up mother's order," Sarah responded. "Mother asked if I wouldn't mind picking it up for her," she explained.

"I decided to take Emma's suggestion and purchase a gift for mother," Benjamin said as he looked at Sarah's beautiful face.

"See, I told you our paths would cross again," Sarah teasingly replied as she recalled their conversation last night at the front door when Benjamin was leaving.

"How fortunate for me," Benjamin fondly said as a warm smile appeared on both their faces. "May I ask for your assistance in helping me to choose a gift for mother?," he asked.

"I'd be glad to make a suggestion. I'm sure you will find something that will be just right," Sarah said.

Benjamin stepped aside and motioned with his hand to allow Sarah to climb the steps to enter Emma's establishment at the Duke of Gloucester Street entrance. When Sarah and Benjamin entered through the doorway, three familiar faces stood staring at them in surprise. Emma, Clarissa and Alexander were standing in the middle of the shop floor with a look of guilt as they all came face to face.

"Hello, what a surprise to see you two," Clarissa awkwardly said.

"Welcome!," Emma quickly replied.

"Hello, Benjamin," Alexander said while Benjamin nodded and began to observe the sleeves of Alexander's tailcoat. "Don't you look lovely today, Sarah," Alexander added in a flattering voice while his eyes appeared hatefully cold.

"Thank you," Sarah replied out of politeness while doubting his sincerity.

"What brings you two in today?," Emma asked while everyone attempted to appear relaxed.

"Mother sent me to pick up her order," Sarah answered.

"I have it packed and ready," Emma informed.

"I decided to take your suggestion and purchase a gift for mother," Benjamin replied to Emma.

"Feel free to look around. I know you will find something that she will love!," Emma responded. "I'll get Caroline's order from the storeroom," she continued while exiting through a door behind the counter.

While Sarah and Benjamin wandered around the shop in search of a gift for Rebecca, Sarah tried to stay focused on their task while she desperately attempted to determine in her mind who's voice she heard on the sidewalk outside. Benjamin discreetly observed Alexander and Clarissa while they uncomfortably stood beside each other on the other side of the room. Benjamin was suddenly taken aback when he noticed a wooden tray resting on one of the display tables against the wall. It contained fancy brass buttons similar to what he had seen on Alexander's sleeves the night before.

"Be sure to tell your mother that a few new hats arrived this morning! I saw a few that I know she will love!," Emma said to Sarah when she returned from the storeroom.

"Emma, these are unusual buttons," Benjamin said as he reached to pick one up from the tray.

"Yes, they are unique, aren't they? My late husband was very fond of that style, so I decided to include them in my inventory," Emma cheerfully replied.

"They are very elegant. James also has a few tailcoats with those type of buttons," Clarissa commented as she and Alexander overheard their conversation while they walked closer to them.

Sarah and Benjamin continued to browse around the shop in an effort to choose the perfect gift for Rebecca. The atmosphere remained tense as Benjamin's mind was distracted by his recent find. Sarah interrupted his puzzled thoughts when she suggested a few items that she thought Rebecca might favor. After deciding on a tortoise shell comb and brush set, they returned to the counter to finalize the purchase.

"Oh, that is beautiful! I know your mother will love it!," Emma exclaimed. "It will take just a moment to wrap it," she continued.

"It is a lovely set," Sarah said as she admired the craftsmanship before Emma placed them in a box.

"Please tell your mother about the lovely hats!," Emma reminded Sarah.

"I'll be sure to tell her. Thank you, Emma," Sarah politely replied while Emma handed her and Benjamin their items.

"You two enjoy the rest of your day," Clarissa said with a forced smile while she continued to stand beside Alexander on the other side of the room.

"It would be my pleasure to escort you home," Benjamin offered as they stepped aside to allow two finely dressed women to enter the shop before he and Sarah closed the door behind them.

"I would like that," Sarah replied with a smile as they descended the steps.

While Sarah and Benjamin quietly strolled along the sidewalk on Duke of Gloucester Street, Sarah continued to silently wonder which female she overheard on the sidewalk while Benjamin silently thought about his earlier suspicions of Alexander and how Alexander seemed to be connected with these two women.

"I enjoyed dinner last night," Benjamin said to break the silence. "It was very nice of you all to invite me," he added.

"I am so glad you accepted. Although, it turned out to be quite an interesting evening," Sarah said.

"Yes, the conversation did take an interesting turn," Benjamin prompted. "I noticed that you and your mother sensed the tension in the conversation," he continued.

"Benjamin, I'm not sure how to tell you this...," Sarah hesitantly said.

"What is it?," Benjamin asked as he saw the look of uncertainty on her face.

"When I was approaching Emma's shop, I heard voices on the sidewalk around the corner on the Botetourt side of the building. I immediately recognized the sound of Alexander's voice, although I was unsure of the female's voice. I was just about to continue around the corner when I heard you call my name. Then, after we entered the shop and the three of them were standing there, I realized it had to be either Emma or Clarissa he was talking to," Sarah said. "They were discussing last night and were wondering if anyone suspected what they were up to," Sarah continued to explain. "I even heard our names mentioned," she added.

"What did they say?," Benjamin anxiously asked.

"Something about us being useful to their plan," Sarah replied.

"That is disturbing. I do not trust that man. I have recently developed suspicions of my own regarding Alexander," Benjamin replied as they continued walking down the sidewalk.

"I noticed that you suddenly became preoccupied last night during dinner," Sarah responded. "Then you seemed troubled the rest of the evening," she continued.

"The morning after our house burned, I found a torn sleeve in the ashes with unique buttons along the sleeve," Benjamin said while trying to forget the painful emotions. "I remember father telling mother and me that someone attacked him from behind when we were fleeing the house as it burned," Benjamin recalled. "I was shocked when I noticed similar buttons on Alexander's sleeve last night but now I'm confused because I just saw similar buttons in Emma's shop," he continued.

"What are you saying?," Sarah gasped as she tried to process Benjamin's revelation.

"I was sure that Alexander caused the fire," Benjamin declared. "But after seeing those buttons in Emma's shop, I realize there could be other possibilities," Benjamin responded.

"Who would do such a thing?," Sarah asked in shock and confusion.

"Whoever it was wanted to cause my family harm," Benjamin firmly stated. "I just need to figure out the killer's motive. I've been trying to think why someone would have a grudge against my family," he added.

"I wonder if it could be Alexander? He has always been jealous of your father and my father too for that matter," Sarah replied. "Wasn't Alexander often defeated in the courtroom when in opposition with your father?," she asked.

"Yes, and I immediately think of the trial of the treasonous Simon Bartram. That trial received a lot of publicity and I heard father speak of it often," Benjamin answered.

"I have heard father speak of it also," Sarah replied. "I was a young girl at the time but I have heard him speak of it occasionally over the years," she continued as she and Benjamin approached the Palace Green and sat on a wooden bench next to the brick sidewalk facing the expansive green space.

While Sarah and Benjamin sat on the bench gazing out across the Palace Green, they continued to sit in silence thinking about the possibilities they had just discussed.

"It seems ironic, but for some reason I just now thought about the carriage accident that happened a few years ago that nearly took our parents' lives," Sarah recalled as she stared at the location of the terrible incident. "I was away at Penderley but when I returned I overheard the servants talking about it. I think mother and father had planned on keeping it from me," she assumed.

"Father told me that his intuition told him that Alexander was somehow involved with that so-called accident," Benjamin replied. "But he never could prove anything," he added.

"Simon Bartram was hung, wasn't he?," Sarah asked.

"Yes. But once I overheard mother and father mention he had a teenage daughter at the time he was executed," Benjamin said.

"I wonder what happened to her?," Sarah pondered.

"She was supposedly placed in the care of a foster family in northern Virginia until she became of age," Benjamin replied.

"Do you think that she would want to harm our families?," Sarah asked with uncertainty.

"I'm not sure. But it's worth considering," Benjamin seriously agreed. "After seeing those buttons for sale in Emma's shop, now I need to consider the possibility of Emma's late husband being a suspect also," Benjamin realized.

"Patrick Adams comes from a very well-respected family. I can't imagine he would do such a thing," Sarah protested. "Any number of men could have bought those buttons. With our fathers' professions, they could have many enemies," she added.

"Maybe I need to find out more about Patrick Adams," Benjamin replied.

"All this makes me wonder about my father's accident," Sarah suspected.

"What accident was that?," Benjamin asked with a surprised look on his face.

"Last summer, he was standing on the sidewalk in front of the Courthouse with a crowd of people and he was suddenly pushed into the street in front of an oncoming carriage," Sarah revealed. "Thankfully, he escaped unharmed with just a few bruises. The driver was able to get the horses under control just in the nick of time," she continued.

"Who pushed him?," Benjamin asked.

"No one knew. It was so crowded and father didn't see who it was because they had approached him from behind," Sarah explained.

"This is making me even more nervous!," Benjamin replied with deep concern. "Now it appears there may be more than one person involved in all of this," Benjamin deducted.

"Do you think it has anything to do with Simon Bartram?," Sarah asked as her mind returned to their earlier conversation. "Wasn't Alexander involved in that trial also?," she continued.

"Yes, Alexander served as Simon's defense attorney and it was rumored that Alexander was also involved in Simon's illegal business dealings," Benjamin explained. "Although, it was rumored there were others also involved," Benjamin added.

"I wonder if Alexander knows what happened to his daughter?," Sarah asked.

"If so, they could have possibly reconnected. She would be in her mid-twenties by now," Benjamin deduced.

"Isn't Emma around that age?," Sarah prompted.

"Yes, and so is Clarissa for that matter. I am becoming suspicious of both of them," Benjamin said.

"I can't imagine someone could harbor such hatred," Sarah said with disbelief.

"It is hard for me to believe also. However, such evil does exist," Benjamin replied while he gazed into Sarah's eyes and admired her innocence.

"We could possibly be in danger!," Sarah responded with serious concern.

"We have to keep our guard up and constantly be aware of our surroundings," Benjamin warned.

"This is all so frightening!," Sarah fearfully said.

"Don't worry, Sarah," Benjamin replied in a comforting voice. "We just have to be careful and everything will be fine," he reassuringly added.

"Do you think we need to tell our parents about our suspicions?," Sarah worriedly inquired.

"I don't think so. We are not sure if any of this is true. We are making a lot of assumptions without any evidence," Benjamin sensibly replied. "Don't worry, Sarah. Everything will be fine," he reassured her again after continuing to see a look of worry on her face.

"I'll trust your prediction that everything will be okay," Sarah said while admiring his confidence. "Thankfully, Father, Mother and I are leaving in a few days for Charles Town to attend my cousin Lucinda's wedding," Sarah added.

"I am returning to Atherton the day after tomorrow. I am going to leave just after sunrise," Benjamin said. "At least your absence will ease my mind since you'll be away from any possible danger in Williamsburg," Benjamin added with relief.

"I will pray for your safety as well," Sarah affectionately responded.

"I would like for you and your parents to join me for supper at Christiana's Tavern tomorrow," Benjamin offered.

"I would like that," Sarah said with a smile as she gazed into his blue eyes.

"I'll present the idea to your parents once I deliver you safely to Hemsworth House," Benjamin teasingly said as they arose from the bench.

As Sarah and Benjamin walked across the Palace Green toward Hemsworth House, they were consumed with their newfound joy in being together even though they were fully aware of the impending danger that may possibly lie ahead.

Charles Town, South Carolina

Late June, 1774

GARY ROWE

Chapter 11

A week earlier, Nathaniel, Thomas and Martha, Ethan and William and their wives and children, traveled from Penderley in Charles City County to Williamsburg to join Lawrence, Caroline and Sarah. After spending two days at Hemsworth House, the Eldridge family boarded a ship at James River Landing to begin their journey to Charles Town. The trip southward began with a cloudless sky and calm waters as the ship sailed down the James River. After a mostly uneventful excursion, except for a stormy evening near the desolate islands off the coast of North Carolina, the ship encountered pleasant weather the following morning as it sailed closer to the South Carolina Colony and into the Charles Town harbor.

Once the Eldridge family had been reunited with the Lockwood's and settled in at Magnolia Grove Plantation, a week of festive social events began in celebration of Lucinda's marriage to Philip Chandler. The Chandler family was well-known throughout the colony and the marriage of Lucinda and Philip would unite the two neighboring rice plantations into a vast and wealthy empire.

A few days after the Eldridge's arrival, an elaborate wedding supper had been planned to provide the initial introduction of both families. Later in the week, an afternoon social was hosted at the Chandler estate for the ladies of both families to become better acquainted and the men gathered at Magnolia Grove to celebrate Philip's last days of bachelorhood.

Two days before the nuptials, the Eldridge ladies spent a leisurely afternoon relaxing on the veranda of Magnolia Grove Plantation. The Eldridge men and Philip Chandler could be heard conversing with occasional laughs through the open windows of the library at the far end of the veranda while they played cards, smoked pipes, and drank George's favorite whiskey that was reserved for very special occasions. The lemony scent that lingered on the breeze from the last blooms of the magnolia trees filled the air on this late June afternoon. A smile formed on Sarah's face as she inhaled the heavenly scent while thoughts of Benjamin and their shared love of nature entered her mind.

"Thank you, Sibby," Lavinia said as the house servant placed a tray filled with small cakes and a pitcher of cider on the table. "We will serve ourselves," Lavinia instructed.

"Yes, ma'am," Sibby politely replied.

"I hope Myles and Michael are not giving you any trouble," Rachel said to Sibby. "Ethan sometimes gets impatient with them and I have to remind him that they are only two-year-old boys," Rachel lightheartedly continued referring to the twins.

"And Phoebe as well," Hannah said to Sibby of her and William's three-year-old daughter.

"I just put them down for a nap...they sleepin' like little angels," Sibby replied.

"Please let us know if they cause you any trouble," Rachel informed as she smiled and then glanced at Hannah.

"Yes, ma'am," Sibby said while she nodded and turned toward the front entrance door.

"Don't you two worry. Sibby is very good with children," Lavinia said to put her two nephew's wives at ease.

"The joys of young motherhood," Martha teasingly said as she smiled at both daughters-in-law. "You'll both worry less when you have a few more," she continued in a more serious tone.

"Martha, I was saddened to hear of your Aunt Verity's passing," Caroline said to her sister-in-law.

"Thank you, Caroline," Martha replied. "I do miss her so very much," she added.

"She was such a kind and loving person," Caroline said. "I'll always remember how she made Lawrence and I feel right at home when we visited," Caroline recalled.

"It's hard to believe that Aunt Verity passed away just a few months after Abigail," Martha said. "It's been difficult for all of us, especially Nathaniel. He and Abigail had such devotion for one another," she continued.

"Yes, they truly were in love. Although, Nathaniel is lucky to have you and Thomas," Caroline said. "As well as Ethan and William and their two lovely wives," Caroline continued as she fondly smiled at Rachel and Hannah.

"I'll never forget Abigail's kindness. She welcomed me into her home with open arms when Ethan began courting me," Rachel shared. "She and Nathaniel both did," she added.

"My mother died when I was young and Abigail was like the mother I never had," Hannah fondly said as she remembered her warmhearted mother-in-law. "I can see where William gets his kind heart from," Hannah affectionately said of her husband's nature.

"We are the lucky ones to have both of you as part of our family," Martha responded. "My boys were blessed when you both came into their lives," she added.

"I am so glad we could all be together for this wonderful occasion," Lavinia cheerfully said.

"We are all so happy for you, Lucinda!," Martha said. "Philip is such a fine young man. The Chandler family is a well-respected and prominent family. You could not have asked for a better union," she continued.

"Thank you, Aunt Martha. I am very happy," Lucinda warmly replied.

"George and I could not be more pleased. We want nothing but happiness for our little girl," Lavinia joyfully said as she smiled at her daughter.

"That is a lovely hat, Aunt Caroline," Lucinda said to divert the attention from herself.

"Thank you! I bought it from my friend Emma who owns a millinery shop in Williamsburg. She has the most adorable things!," Caroline replied. "She and I have become such good friends in such short amount of time," Caroline added.

Sarah worriedly looked at her mother wondering if she should tell her about her recent suspicions of Emma.

"I always remember how much you love hats," Martha added to the conversation.

"Yes, mother does have a fondness for them," Sarah said.

"How is your friend, Jane?," Caroline asked Martha. "I remember when we visited her shop in Petersburg. She had some very nice things!," Caroline recalled.

"She has done quite well for herself. She is still running a successful business and has become well-known throughout the area," Martha informed.

"Whatever happened to that unruly girl that Jane and her husband were looking after?," Caroline asked. "After all this time, I still remember how rude she was that time we visited Jane's millinery shop during Christmas," she continued.

"Yes, but they did not keep her long. That awful girl was so ungrateful and she was more than Jane could handle. The authorities placed her with another family," Martha explained.

"Why was she placed with another family?," Sarah asked as her interest grew.

"Jane found out that the girl's father was convicted of a crime and was executed," Martha informed. "And the girl had no other family," she continued.

"You never mentioned that to me before. That sounds like it could be Simon Bartram," Caroline replied.

"Yes, it does sound similar. Although, I thought I told you that a long time ago," Martha surprisingly said.

"What was her name?," Sarah asked as she intently listened to their conversation while the mention of a millinery shop and Simon Bartram made her think of Emma.

"It's strange, but I don't recall. I'm not sure if I ever heard Jane mention her name," Martha replied. "Jane and her husband were relieved when the authorities found her another home," she continued.

"How old was she?," Sarah inquired.

"I believe I heard Jane mention she was around fifteen when they took her in. I'm sure she's in her early twenties by now," Martha answered.

Sarah immediately thought of her and Benjamin's conversation from the week before as they sat on the bench overlooking the Palace Green. For some reason, the mention of a millinery shop and Simon Bartram made her think of Emma. She also remembered that Benjamin said Simon Bartram's daughter was placed in a foster home. However, she realized she knew very little about Emma's background. While Sarah was deep in thought, she hardly noticed the magnolia trees that she loved so much as she stared out over the front lawn. The sight of those wonderful trees would normally bring her excitement but on this occasion her mind was heavily occupied with her and Benjamin's recent revelations. Sarah suddenly realized how lonely she felt without Benjamin being near.

"Sarah, I hear you have won the attention of a very eligible and handsome man," Martha teased as if she was reading Sarah's thoughts.

"Oh, Aunt Martha!," Sarah replied while the ladies looked toward the front entrance door as Lawrence and George walked onto the veranda to join the ladies.

"Did you two men escape from that rowdy bunch?," Caroline laughingly teased.

"Yes, things were getting a little too wild for me," Lawrence jokingly replied.

"Those rascals ate all of our cake," George said with a smile as he reached for one of the leftover cakes on the tray on the nearby table.

"What are you ladies talking about?," Lawrence asked as he sat down in the empty chair beside Caroline.

"We are learning about the man who has taken an interest in Sarah," Martha explained while Sarah sighed with embarrassment.

"Don't be modest, Sarah," Caroline said to her daughter. "Benjamin Thompson of Atherton County has taken an interest in our little girl," Caroline happily said as she glanced at Lawrence.

"His grandfather was General Robert Atherton who founded Atherton Village," Lavinia said for the benefit of Rachel and Hannah as she glanced in their direction.

"Lawrence and I were very close to his parents, Rebecca and John Thompson," Caroline said. "John passed away a couple of years ago," she added. "It was very tragic. Both John and General Atherton died in the fire that destroyed their home."

"I can't imagine the pain that Rebecca and Benjamin must have felt," Lavinia sympathetically said.

"Yes, and to make it worse there were suspicious circumstances surrounding that tragedy," Lawrence responded.

"Did I hear someone say that an intruder in the house attacked John from behind and a candle that fell to the floor started the fire?," George asked.

"Yes, but no one ever became a suspect and nothing else was discovered," Lawrence said as Sarah immediately thought of the torn sleeve that Benjamin found in the ashes of the fire.

"Wasn't it rumored that Alexander Drake may have been somehow been involved?," George asked.

"That has been said. Although, no one ever tried to prove anything," Lawrence replied.

"My good friend Emma has taken a liking to Alexander and I can't imagine what she sees in him," Caroline said. "I just can't imagine what would draw those two together and why they would be associating with one another," Caroline continued as she wondered out loud.

"I have thought about that myself," Lawrence said as he glanced at Caroline.

"As much as I dislike that man, I care very much about Emma and hope that she will come to her senses on her own," Caroline optimistically said.

"He is rather sly. Although, I can see how he could easily fool someone who doesn't know him that well with his fake charm," Sarah said. "Father, can you think of any other enemies that John may have had besides Alexander?," Sarah asked.

"I'm sure that John had other enemies due to his profession as a prosecuting lawyer," Lawrence answered.

Sarah sat quietly in her chair contemplating all that she had just heard. The mention of the unruly foster girl, a millinery shop and Emma's association with Alexander brought her to believe that Emma could possibly be Simon Bartram's daughter. Also, Emma's current age coincided with Sarah's new theory and made her suspicions even more probable.

"Enough about this unpleasant subject," Lavinia lightheartedly said while she interrupted Sarah's thoughts. "Let's talk about the happy occasion that we are all here for!," Lavinia merrily added.

While the conversation began to take a lighter turn, Philip led the way through the front door as the other men joined the rest of the family on the veranda. As Sarah sat quietly in her chair, she immediately noticed Lucinda's eyes begin to sparkle as soon as she saw Philip walk through the door. When Sarah observed Philip display a similar reaction at the sight of Lucinda, she instinctively knew the happy couple was truly in love as she watched their faces light up with the sight of one another.

"I see you men decided to take a break too," Lavinia said with a laugh as she saw the men walk through the front door. "Father, come sit by me," see continued as she glanced at Nathaniel as the men walked toward them.

"Your father is too old for this kind of activity!," Nathaniel jokingly said to his daughter as he began to sit in the chair beside Lavinia.

"It will keep you young!," Lavinia affectionately replied as she laid her hand on Nathaniel's wrist while it rested on the arm of the chair next to her.

"That's exactly what I told him," Thomas teasingly said of his father as he sat down in the settee beside Martha.

"How would you two ladies like to take a stroll under the magnolia trees?" Ethan said as he and William glanced at Rachel and Hannah.

"That would be lovely!," Hannah said, answering for both herself and Rachel as they arose from their chairs.

As Sarah watched Ethan and William romantically stroll arm-in-arm with their wives across the front lawn, it was obvious that they too had found true love. While Sarah continued to observe the happy couples walk under the majestic magnolia trees, a warm smile appeared on her face as her thoughts wandered to the handsome man of Atherton County who had captured her heart.

Two days later, on the morning of Lucinda and Philip's wedding, the sun brightly arose in the early summer sky while a light breeze carried the faint scent of magnolia blossoms through the air. In the presence of nearly one-hundred guests, Lucinda and Philip exchanged vows on the front lawn of Magnolia Grove Plantation underneath the towering magnolia trees. While Sarah happily watched her cousin Lucinda in her beautiful white dress marrying the man of her dreams, her thoughts joyfully wandered to her childhood years when she first dreamed about her own wedding day carrying a bouquet of magnolia blossoms as she walked down the aisle.

GARY ROWE

Atherton County, Virginia

Late June, 1774

GARY ROWE

Chapter 12

Benjamin felt a sigh of relief as he rode Thunder through the entrance gates of Atherton Hall. As the evening approached and the sun dropped below the clouds along the horizon, Thunder eagerly galloped down the long path toward the house after he and Benjamin's tiring return from Williamsburg. Even though Benjamin was glad to return to the familiarity of his beloved home, he felt an emptiness in his heart as he thought about the beautiful girl he had left behind. However, he was relieved that Sarah and her parents would be away from danger while they attended her cousin's wedding in Charles Town.

The following morning, when Benjamin awakened in his mahogany four poster bed, the early morning sunlight filtered into his dimly lit bedchamber through the cracks in the wooden shutters that hung at the windows. After getting out of bed and walking to one of the windows, he reached for the knobs on each wooden panel and folded them back into each side of the window casing to allow the sunlight to brighten the room. While Benjamin stood gazing out over the front lawn of Atherton Hall and down toward the river, the picturesque scene made him temporarily forget about the heavy burden that was on his mind. As he admired the morning sunlight that glistened off the rippling waters of the river and his young magnolia trees along the river's edge, the tranquility and beauty of the peaceful scene reminded him of Sarah.

After an early morning ride into the fields to inspect his tobacco crop, and being pleased with what he saw, Benjamin returned to the house in hopes of joining his mother for breakfast. When Benjamin found the dining room empty, he realized that his visit to the fields took longer than expected. Once Benjamin had finished his cup of coffee and a bowl of cornmeal porridge, he wandered into the front parlor to find his mother reading a book in the comfort of her favorite wing chair while Horace was comfortably curled up on the floor beside her. As soon as he entered the doorway, Horace raised his head off the floor and began wagging his tail at the sight of Benjamin.

"Good morning, mother," Benjamin said with a smile as he walked toward her and bent forward to kiss her on the cheek. "I missed you at breakfast," he continued while reaching to pet Horace on the top of his head.

"I see you arose early. I thought you might sleep a little later this morning after your tiring journey," Rebecca said to her son as she laid the book in her lap while Horace resumed his comfortable position on the floor.

"I wanted to inspect the fields this morning," Benjamin replied. "The tobacco crop is coming along nicely," he continued while he sat in the other wing chair opposite his mother.

"We should have a good yield this year," Rebecca agreed. "How was your time in Williamsburg?," she asked.

"The merchant's meeting was a success. But not without its usual disagreements and conflicts upon participants," Benjamin truthfully answered. "By the way, Thomas Jefferson asked me to give you his regards. He also expressed his condolences over father and grandfather's passing," Benjamin informed his mother.

"That was very kind of him. He is a thoughtful young man," Rebecca said as she recalled seeing him on several occasions when she had traveled to Williamsburg with John on business.

"And the Eldridge's sent their love. They made me feel right at home during my visit," Benjamin informed.

"I can see by the smile on your face that you enjoyed seeing Sarah," Rebecca responded after noticing the expression of happiness on her son's face.

"I do enjoy being in her presence," Benjamin replied. "We have much in common. And I have never felt this way before," Benjamin continued.

"Benjamin, I am very happy for you! Sarah comes from a highly respected family and nothing would make me happier than for you to find true love," Rebecca said.

"I think I am in love," Benjamin replied as a vision of Sarah appeared in his mind. "I am looking forward to seeing her again," he continued with anticipation.

"You will definitely get to see her during our celebration in a few weeks," Rebecca reminded.

"Yes, that has been on my mind," Benjamin replied as he thought about he and Sarah's suspicions.

"I need to send out the last of the invitations," Rebecca said. "I received a letter yesterday from Naomi Prescott expressing her happiness for our accomplishment of restoring the Atherton home," she continued. "Naomi, James and Clarissa are thrilled to accept our invitation and are looking forward to our celebration," she continued. "She received the invitation the day James and Clarissa returned from Williamsburg. Naomi mentioned in her letter that James and Clarissa had the pleasure of your company at the Eldridge's."

"Yes, they joined us for supper. James's wife is very attractive," Benjamin said.

"Naomi keeps me informed through our frequent letters but I have never had the opportunity to meet Clarissa in person," Rebecca responded.

"Mother, what do you know about Clarissa Prescott?," Benjamin asked.

"Why do you ask?," Rebecca inquired.

"I met Clarissa when I joined the Eldridges for supper," Benjamin answered. "She and James seem an unlikely pair," he continued.

"I do know that Naomi was surprised when James married her," Rebecca said, recalling a past conversation with James's mother. "She felt that James didn't take the time to get to know her very well before marrying her. From my understanding, Clarissa hasn't been very forthcoming about her past," Rebecca informed.

"During supper, I heard James mention that Clarissa was originally from the northern part of Virginia," Benjamin said.

"I recall Naomi mentioning that. She also said that Clarissa is a widow," Rebecca replied. "However, that is all that Naomi knows about her," she added. "Edward would roll over in his grave if he knew his son did not marry someone from his same social standing," Rebecca said knowing how Edward Prescott felt about marrying within one's class.

"How long have Clarissa and James been married?," Benjamin asked.

"I believe it has been a little over two years," Rebecca recalled.

"I got the feeling that Clarissa and Alexander Drake know each other," Benjamin said.

"What does Alexander have to do with anything?," Rebecca asked.

"He was also a guest of the Eldridges," Benjamin said as he saw a look of shock on his mother's face. "Not directly. Remember when Mrs. Eldridge informed us that her friend Emma wasn't sure who would be her escort?," Benjamin asked. "It was Alexander. I got the feeling that everyone was shocked when the two of them showed up together," he continued.

"I can't imagine Caroline and Lawrence having that man in their home," Rebecca shocking said.

"I'm sure they tolerate him for the sake of their friendship with Emma," Benjamin replied. "Emma is being courted by Alexander," he informed.

"Oh that poor girl! Does she know what type of man she is involved with?," Rebecca asked in shock. "I would hope not," she added while thinking of the poor girl's ignorance while Benjamin was thinking just the opposite.

"Emma was married to a man named Patrick Adams," Benjamin said as he recalled the conversation during supper. "She mentioned being a widow before she married him," he added.

"Oh, I didn't realize when Caroline said she had a friend named Emma that was who she was referring to. I do not know much about the Adams family except that they are extremely wealthy," Rebecca said. "I can't imagine her wanting to run a millinery shop with her inherited wealth," she added.

"I heard her mention she always wanted to own a millinery shop since she was a young girl," Benjamin informed. "Now I understand why she carries such high-end and expensive merchandise," he continued while recalling the fine quality of her goods.

"Our friends, the Baldwin's, know more about the Adams family," Rebecca said. "It seems I recall Penelope Baldwin mentioning that Patrick Adams passed away. I believe that was about two years ago," she added.

"I would like to invite Emma Adams to our celebration," Benjamin said, thinking the opportunity would allow him to learn more about her involvement with Alexander. "Would you be upset if she invited Alexander as her escort?," Benjamin asked while realizing the possibility.

"Benjamin!," Rebecca responded in shock. "How could think about having that man in our home?," she asked in bewilderment.

"Mrs. Eldridge and Emma have become close friends. I don't want to offend her by not inviting Emma," Benjamin said as an excuse to further the investigation of his and Sarah's suspicions, while Rebecca searchingly observed her son knowing there must be an important motive behind his request.

"Well, I'll trust you to make the right decision," Rebecca replied as she wondered what her son may not be telling her, while Benjamin wondered if he should confide in his mother but decided against giving her cause to worry.

"When I return to Williamsburg the week after next, I'll hand deliver their invitations," Benjamin said with a comforting smile in hopes of putting his mother at ease.

Later that night, while Benjamin climbed the staircase in the front entrance hall to retire for the evening, thoughts of the conversation he had with his mother earlier in the morning entered his mind. His gut instinct told him there was more to James and Clarissa Prescott than met the eye. An uneasy feeling overcame him as he considered the possibility they were somehow linked to

Emma Adams and Alexander Drake. He just had to figure out how.

As he walked down the upstairs hallway pondering over his thoughts, a vision of Sarah appeared in his mind. Benjamin realized how eager he was to return to Williamsburg. Once he entered his dimly lit bedchamber, he instantly wandered to the window to gaze out over the front lawn once again. The bright moonlight in the early summer sky cast a romantic glow over the familiar landscape. For a short while, Benjamin stood admiring the romantic scene before reaching to light the chamberstick that sat on top of his writing desk near the window. After slowly opening one of the drawers, he pulled a piece of paper from the compartment and sat comfortably in the chair. Benjamin slid the inkwell closer and reached for the quill.

21 June, 1774

Dear Sarah,

I hope my letter finds you well and will be waiting for you upon your return to Virginia. I will be returning to Williamsburg on the 3rd of July for a couple of days and hope to see you during my visit.

I have learned a few more details regarding our recent discoveries and look forward to sharing them with you.

As I rode through the gates of Atherton Hall upon my return from Williamsburg, the sight of the magnolia trees reminded me of your innocence and grace and our shared

love of nature's never-ending beauty.
I pray for your safety until we meet again.

Yours truly,
Benjamin

Benjamin smiled as he neatly folded the parchment paper and placed a dab of wax on the overlapping edge before pressing his stamp into the wax to seal the letter. After arising from his chair and wandering to his bedside, he blew out the candle in the chamberstick and placed it on the table beside his bed. While he slowly fell into a peaceful slumber, Benjamin began to dream of a particular young lady as they strolled arm-in-arm under the magnolia trees alongside the river.

Williamsburg, Virginia

Early July, 1774

GARY ROWE

Chapter 13

Benjamin arrived in Williamsburg during late afternoon on an unusually warm day in early July. As he and Thunder rode into town, a much-welcomed breeze began to stir as the sun lowered in the cloudless sky. When he arrived at his usual resting place, Benjamin found Christiana Campbell's Tavern to be a more peaceful and quieter place than his earlier trip three weeks prior for the Meeting of the Merchants. After enjoying a relaxing meal in the tavern's dining room, he returned to his room with hopes of having a restful night. Feeling somewhat recuperated, he arose early the next morning to attend to his usual business. During his walk across town to settle his accounts with a few merchants, Benjamin took the opportunity to make a quick stop by

Emma's shop to present her with an invitation to the Atherton celebration.

"Benjamin!," Emma said in surprise as he entered through the doorway from the Botetourt Street entrance. "What a nice surprise!," she continued as she walked from behind the counter to greet him. "What brings you back to town so soon?"

"I'm attending to regular business but while I was in town I wanted to take the opportunity to present you with an invitation to Atherton Hall," Benjamin said while handing her an envelope embossed with the Atherton family crest. "Mother and I are hosting an affair to celebrate the completion of our home. We have planned games, plenty of good food and a fancy dance on the last night. And, of course, we have accommodations for our out-of-town guests," he explained.

"Oh, how thoughtful!," Emma responded as she glanced at the envelope after taking it with her hand. "I have been excited to see your home for myself after hearing about it when we joined the Eldridges for supper," she continued.

"Thank you, Emma. Of course, the invitation is for you and your escort," Benjamin said as Alexander unexpectedly appeared in the doorway from the Duke of Gloucester Street entrance.

"My escort has just arrived!," Emma smiled as Alexander gave her a puzzled look.

"Benjamin," Alexander cordially said while nodding his head in acknowledgement.

"Alexander," Benjamin coolly replied while trying to hide his dislike towards this man.

"Benjamin has invited us to a celebration at Atherton Hall!," Emma excitedly said to Alexander as he walked to join them while they stood beside the sales counter.

"I hear it is quite impressive," Alexander said with an undertone of envy as he stood beside Emma.

"Benjamin, I hope your mother liked the comb and brush set you picked out for her," Emma said as she remembered his purchase.

"Yes, very much so. She was delighted with its beauty and quality," Benjamin replied.

"I am so happy that she was pleased," Emma responded. "I only like to carry quality merchandise," she proudly added.

"You do have a nice shop," Benjamin replied. "Well, please don't let me interrupt your day any longer," he added. "Mother and I look forward to seeing you both at our event," Benjamin continued as he turned toward the door.

"Yes! We are looking forward to it!," Emma eagerly responded for both her and Alexander. "Thank you again for inviting us!," she excitedly said while Benjamin turned to suspiciously look back at them after reaching the door to the Duke of Gloucester Street entrance.

"Good day to you both," Benjamin politely said with a nod as he exited through the shop door.

While Benjamin continued down the brick sidewalk on Duke of Gloucester Street toward the west side of town, his intuition told him that Emma and Alexander were not exactly who they presented themselves to be. Benjamin had an uneasy feeling they were somehow linked to the misfortunes of his own family as well as the Eldridges. On his way across town, he was temporarily distracted from his suspicions while he visited a few local merchants to conduct business. After settling his accounts and placing a few new orders, Benjamin decided to make a final stop at the courthouse with hopes of seeing Lawrence. Once he crossed the street, after pausing to let a carriage pass, he spoke to a few familiar people standing on the sidewalk in front of the courthouse as he approached the steps to the building. When Benjamin reached for the handle to one of the double doors to enter the courthouse, he almost collided with Lawrence as he was exiting the building.

"Benjamin, what a nice surprise!," Lawrence happily said as he came to a sudden halt in the doorway to avoid running into him. "When did you get into town?," he asked.

"I arrived late yesterday afternoon," Benjamin answered. "I took care of a few business matters today and I thought I would take the chance to see if you were here," he continued.

"I was just about to leave for the day," Lawrence said. "Why don't you walk home with me. Caroline and Sarah would be delighted to see you," he continued.

"Thank you, I'd like that," Benjamin happily replied while hoping he would see Sarah.

After walking a few blocks northward, and taking a glimpse over the brick wall to admire Bruton Parish Church along the way, Benjamin glanced toward the other side of the street across the Palace Green as they approached the Eldridge home and was reminded of the carriage accident that he and Sarah discussed during his last visit.

Once he and Lawrence entered the entrance hall to Hemsworth House, Benjamin discreetly smiled as his thoughts turned to Sarah.

"Look who I ran into!," Lawrence announced as he and Benjamin entered the front parlor to find Caroline and Sarah playing a game of backgammon while sitting at a game table in a corner of the room.

"Benjamin, please come in!," Caroline said in surprise as she and Sarah looked up from the board game.

"Please don't let me interrupt your game," Benjamin apologetically replied as Caroline arose from her chair to greet him, while he and Sarah glanced at each other and shared an intimate smile.

"Sarah is certainly on a winning streak," Caroline teased while fondly glancing at her daughter.

"Hello, Sarah," Benjamin warmly said as Sarah arose from her chair.

"It's nice to see you, Benjamin," Sarah warmly replied.

"While I was in town, I wanted to personally deliver your invitation to our celebration at Atherton Hall," Benjamin said to the Eldridges as he reached to retrieve the envelope from his coat pocket.

"Oh, how wonderful!," Caroline exclaimed as Benjamin handed her the invitation. "Atherton Hall is lovely! And it will be nice to see Rebecca again," she continued.

"Yes, we are looking forward to it," Lawrence said as he glanced at Sarah, knowing his daughter was pleased as well.

"Please sit down, Benjamin," Caroline said. "May we offer you some refreshment?," she asked.

"Thank you, but no," Benjamin replied. "I probably should be on my way," he added.

"There is no need to rush," Lawrence said to Benjamin.

"It's such a lovely day. Why don't you and Sarah take a walk in the gardens," Caroline prompted as she smiled at her daughter and then glanced at Benjamin. "My roses are in full bloom and the scent is heavenly!," she proudly added.

"It would be my pleasure," Benjamin replied to Caroline and then turned his head to glance at Sarah.

"That would be nice," Sarah replied as she gazed into his blue eyes.

"Well, you two enjoy yourselves," Caroline said.

As Benjamin and Sarah turned toward the entrance hall, Caroline warmly smiled at Lawrence acknowledging the happiness their daughter had found.

While Benjamin escorted Sarah through the center hall toward the rear entrance door, they both quietly relished in their joy at seeing each other once again. After

Benjamin opened the door for Sarah to step over the threshold onto the stoop, they descended the brick steps together while their senses were met by the fragrance of roses filling the afternoon air.

"Your mother was right! The roses do smell heavenly," Benjamin said as he slowly inhaled the sweet scent and admired the bushes along the brick walkway filled with pink and white blossoms and many newly formed buds.

While the happy couple strolled along the brick pathway, laid in the symmetrical pattern of a formal English-style garden, they silently enjoyed each other's company and the sights and sounds of nature's beauty. Hollyhocks in shades of pink, purple and yellow, Stokes' aster in rich shades of blue and white garden phlox were surrounded by perfectly manicured English boxwood hedges that lined the borders of each grid between the brick paths.

As Sarah and Benjamin approached a wooden bench along the fence that lined the outer perimeter of the garden, they paused to enjoy the shade from the branches of the pink crepe myrtle trees that had been planted along the edge of the garden to create a private and intimate setting. Sarah and Benjamin were suddenly startled when two red cardinals abruptly flew out of the trees.

"It looks as if we have invaded their privacy," Benjamin laughingly said while they stopped on the pathway in front of the bench.

"It seems so," Sarah responded as she laughed along with him while they both sat down to enjoy the shade and escape the heat from the afternoon sun. "I'm sure they'll find another resting place somewhere else," she lightheartedly continued.

"Sarah, I've missed spending time with you," Benjamin affectionately said.

"I feel the same way, Benjamin," Sarah fondly responded as she leaned towards him. "I enjoyed receiving your letter. I've been thinking a lot about our previous conversation," she continued.

"I've been thinking about it too. I visited Emma earlier today at her shop," Benjamin said. "I hand delivered her invitation to the Atherton celebration," Benjamin continued.

"I wonder if she will invite Alexander to be her escort?," Sarah asked.

"She already has asked him. He happened to walk through the door when I was there," Benjamin answered.

"Will James and Clarissa be attending?," Sarah inquired.

"Mother received a letter from James's mother the day before I returned home saying James, Clarissa and his mother have accepted our invitation and will be attending," Benjamin informed.

"Since both couples will be there, hopefully it will give us the opportunity to find out more information," Sarah deducted. "Although, I have an uneasy feeling that we could possibly be in danger," she fearfully added.

"I thought of that too. But don't worry, there will be a lot of people attending so we will be safe," Benjamin assured.

"Knowing that makes me feel a little safer," Sarah said as she admired his courage.

"I asked mother if she knew anything about Clarissa Prescott," Benjamin prompted.

"What did she say?," Sarah asked.

"Mother told me that Clarissa and James have been married for about two years," Benjamin informed. "And that Clarissa has not been very forthcoming about her past," he continued.

"By the way, James and Clarissa are in town," Sarah said. "I heard father mention something about James taking care of some business at the courthouse," she added.

"I wonder if Clarissa could be Bartram's daughter?," Benjamin prompted as he thought about the similarities between her and Emma.

"We could be in danger at Atherton Hall if she is Bartram's daughter!" Sarah said as she considered the possibility.

"Yes, and even more so if James is involved in their plan," Benjamin replied as he remembered Clarissa's comment about James having similar buttons like the ones for sale in Emma's shop.

"I just can't believe that James could be involved in any kind of wrongdoing," Sarah responded. "He is such a sweet and kind man," she continued.

"I agree. He has always appeared to be that way. Mother also said that Penelope Baldwin told her that Emma has been a widow for nearly two years," Benjamin said to consider all the facts.

"When you walked me home after our visit to Emma's shop, I forgot to mention the note that Emma sent mother earlier in the morning thanking mother for her hospitality," Sarah said.

"What was unusual about that?," Benjamin asked.

"She signed the note with a middle initial of 'B'," Sarah answered. "Could that stand for Bartram?," she asked.

"That certainly could be a possibility," Benjamin said as an expression of surprise and dismay appeared on his face. "And it would explain her association with Alexander," he continued.

"And in her note she said she especially enjoyed meeting you," Sarah said.

"I guess that could be an innocent comment or have a hidden meaning," Benjamin replied. "We'll have to find out what the initial 'B' stands for," he continued.

THE MAGNOLIAS OF ATHERTON HALL

"When we were in Charles Town, the conversation of Simon Bartram just happened to come up one day when my family was talking," Sarah said.

"Did you learn anything new?," Benjamin asked.

"My Aunt Martha mentioned an incident nearly ten years ago when she and mother visited her Aunt Verity in Petersburg," Sarah explained. "Aunt Martha and mother visited a millinery shop owned by Aunt Martha's friend Jane. Jane and her husband had just taken in a foster girl that was angry and rude. That was around the time of the trial. Do you think it is just a coincidence or could that have possibly been Simon Bartram's daughter?," Sarah asked.

"Did they mention her name?," Benjamin inquired.

"I asked that question but neither Aunt Martha or mother knew her name," Sarah explained.

"Didn't Emma mention she worked in a millinery shop when she was a young girl?," Benjamin asked.

"She did!," Sarah worriedly replied as she recalled the conversation.

"I told mother I was going to invite Emma to our celebration at Atherton Hall and it may be a possibility she would invite Alexander to be her escort," Benjamin said.

"How did she react?," Sarah asked.

"She wasn't happy with the idea but she said it was up to me," Benjamin explained. "I almost told her of our suspicions. But I decided it would be best not to worry her," Benjamin continued.

"I agree. I have said nothing to Mother and Father," Sarah replied.

"The only way to solve this mystery is to get all of them together and discreetly ask questions," Benjamin said. "Maybe someone will reveal something by accident," Benjamin added.

"I just want this to be over. I am afraid for all of us," Sarah frightfully said.

"Don't worry, Sarah. Everything will be fine," Benjamin warmly replied to put her at ease while they gazed into each other's eyes.

"I believe you," Sarah responded as she realized her feelings for him grew deeper each time they were together.

"Did you enjoy your cousin's wedding?," Benjamin asked to steer the conversation in a more pleasant direction.

"Lucinda was a beautiful bride. She and Philip are very happy," Sarah answered. "They were married on the front lawn of Magnolia Grove Plantation. It was a beautiful day and the last of the magnolias were in bloom," she joyfully reminisced.

"I know you enjoyed that!," Benjamin replied while being reminded of her love for the magnificent flower. "It sounds like a perfect ceremony," he added.

"Ever since I was a child, I have dreamed of a similar wedding," Sarah confided with a warm smile.

"Sometimes dreams have a way of coming true!," Benjamin teasingly replied as he stood and extended his hand.

"Yes!," Sarah happily replied while she took his hand. "I believe dreams really do come true," she continued as they happily strolled toward the house.

Chapter 14

On the west side of town, a block east of Emma's shop, a young woman sat on a wooden bench facing Botetourt Street along the brick wall that surrounded the Capitol building. The light afternoon breeze provided a comfortable resting place as it rustled the leaves on the branches of the oak trees that hung overhead. As people occasionally passed by on the sidewalk, the brown-haired beauty politely spoke and anyone observing her presence would never imagine anything out of the ordinary while she comfortably relaxed on the bench. As she sat in solitude enjoying the pleasant summer day, she gradually became preoccupied when her thoughts began to focus on her true intentions.

Eventually the wheels of an approaching coach and the clatter of horses' hooves on the street caused her to suddenly look upward when they interrupted her thoughts. The startling but expected noise reminded her of why she was at this location during this particular time of day. The driver of the coach drove the horses along the curb when the passenger inside instructed him to come to a halt in front of the bench. The passenger slowly reached out the window of the coach with his left hand motioning for her to join him inside. When she recognized the occupant's sleeve with its unique buttons, she willingly arose from the bench. He politely opened the door to allow her to enter, and after accepting his hand to assist her inside, she comfortably settled into the black leather seat opposite him inside the coach.

"I see you received my note," he calmly said.

"He had business to attend to in court. So, it provided me with an opportunity to slip away unnoticed," she informed.

"I'm glad you could join me," he said with lust in his eyes while taking the opportunity to admire her female figure.

"Now that we have both been invited to Atherton Hall, this will provide us with an excellent opportunity," she connivingly said while her mind was focused on more serious matters. "This time we cannot make any mistakes!," she added with determination.

"Don't worry, this time it won't fail," he assuredly replied while her fierce demeanor caused him to focus on the true purpose of their meeting.

"It better not! There have been too many failed attempts!," she angrily responded.

"It's not my fault that luck has constantly been on his side," he said in defense. "I was sure the man I hired to push the Judge in the street in front of that oncoming carriage would have taken care of him," he said to remind her of his efforts.

"Well, it obviously did not!," she said in frustration. "The man you hired must have been an idiot! That was not a difficult task," she angrily said.

"I thought the carriage accident would have taken care of all of them at one time," he continued.

"They were all lucky," she replied in frustration. "Except for the unfortunate fate of John Thompson," she continued as a wicked smile appeared on her face.

"That did turn out better than we expected, didn't it?," he proudly said. "Although, his wife and son got lucky," he said in disappointment.

"Now that we have gotten into their inner circle, this will give us an even better opportunity," she responded. "They have to pay for what they did to me!," she passionately continued.

"The Judge's luck is coming to an end," he said to calm her down.

"That's what you told me this past Christmas when the fox hunt accident failed," she replied to remind him of another failed attempt.

"It wasn't my fault the gun jammed!," he responded while recalling his frustration as he hid in the woods of the Penderley estate as the hunting party rode by.

"This time it cannot fail!," she desperately exclaimed. "You know you want them to pay for how they have treated you!," she continued, reminding him of his hatred toward them.

"Yes, they have to pay for what they have done to both of us!," he replied as he focused on his jealousy and resentment.

"Harming Sarah would be a good way to bring Lawrence Eldridge the pain he deserves," she evilly said.

"It's a shame to hurt such a pretty little creature," the man replied.

"Yes, but that will make Lawrence Eldridge's pain much deeper," she said with satisfaction.

"I'm sure Benjamin will be by her side most of the time," he assumed.

"Well if he gets in the way, we can take care of him too!," she retorted.

"Don't' worry, you have my word they will all be taken care of," he responded with confidence.

"Once this is done, nothing will stop us from being together," she deceptively replied.

"I want to feel you in my arms," he passionately said while his eyes traveled over the sensuous lips on her seductive face and down to the flawless skin at her neckline just above the rise of her breasts.

"There will be plenty of time for that, my love," the female seductively said when she saw the look in his eyes.

"You know what you do to me, don't you?," he lustfully said while arising from his seat in an attempt to join her on the other side of the coach.

"We'll have plenty of time for that later. I have to be going," she worriedly said as she quickly arose from her seat. "I don't want to be missed," she continued to stop him from joining her.

"I'll meet you at the shop tomorrow," he responded as he sat back down on his seat while she reached for the latch on the coach door.

As Simon Bartram's daughter left the interior of the coach, she discreetly turned her head to look in both directions before stepping onto the sidewalk. Once she was satisfied that no one was watching, she turned around to face the coach and gave her lover a seductive glance through the window.

When she turned to walk down the sidewalk, her thoughts began to focus on the revenge she had so desperately sought for so many years and she joyfully relished in the fact that all of her efforts were finally going to come true. Those two conceited men had to pay for the hardships she endured by the loss of her father's finances and the comfortable lifestyle she lost as a young girl. With all the setbacks she encountered, she had no intent of giving up now.

After eliminating two husbands to achieve her goal, she knew this final act would satisfy her thirst for revenge even though she had regained her wealth from her choice of husbands. Once her desires were accomplished, she would settle into her comfortable life and no one would ever know of her illustrious past.

As she continued down the sidewalk, speaking to an occasional person that passed by, her thoughts wandered to Alexander. For a brief moment, she almost felt sorry for him because she knew he had no idea that she had no intention of spending her life with him. Alexander could never be part of the aristocracy due to his bloodline and could never satisfy her lust for social status and the privileges and admiration that were associated with it. He was just a means to an end and a useful tool to help her accomplish her goal. Once the deed was done and she had finished using him as a pawn for her revenge, she would let him take the blame. In feigned innocence, she would retreat back to her comfortable and secure aristocratic lifestyle.

As the man watched Simon Bartram's daughter walk down the street from the window of the coach, he lustfully assessed her from head to toe as he gazed at the seductive figure continuing down the sidewalk. Making love to this beautiful creature had a control over him like no other woman he had ever known before. With lust in his eyes and the soon to be taste of victory on his tongue, he reached out the window to motion the driver to move ahead.

GARY ROWE

THE MAGNOLIAS OF ATHERTON HALL

Atherton County, Virginia

Late July, 1774

GARY ROWE

Chapter 15

When the sound of the horses and the wheels of the approaching coaches could be heard on the pathway in front of the house, Horace raised his head off the floor while resting in his usual spot in the back part of the front entrance hall. Once the canine realized what he heard, he immediately arose from the floor.

"Are the rooms all prepared?," Rebecca asked while she stood at the base of the stairs in the front entrance hall.

"Yes, ma'am," Tula replied.

"Please take one more look to make sure," Rebecca suggested.

"Yes, ma'am," Tula replied once again as she heeded to her mistress's suggestion and began to ascend the steps.

"Easy, boy!," Benjamin called after Horace as the canine darted through the front entrance hall passed Rebecca and toward the front door. "I'm excited too!," Benjamin said as he appeared from the back of the entrance hall while the canine excitedly wagged his tail and scratched at the door.

"It looks like our out of town guests are here," Rebecca said as she turned to watch Benjamin reach for the doorknob to let Horace outside.

As the Eldridge and Prescott coaches came to a halt in front of the house, Horace raced ahead of Benjamin and Rebecca as they descended the steps of the portico to greet their arriving guests. The long-anticipated celebration of the completion of the rebuilding of the Atherton family home had finally arrived.

Benjamin hesitantly left Williamsburg behind two weeks prior to the celebration at Atherton Hall. He had an uneasy feeling of fear for Sarah and her family. However, the preparations for the upcoming celebration at Atherton Hall and the hope of seeing Sarah again in just a short time served as a diversion to help ease his worries.

A week after Benjamin's departure, Sarah's face lit up when she received a letter with the familiar Atherton imprint on the wax seal. Her heart fluttered as she read Benjamin's words. His concern for her and her family's safety, his admiration of her kind and caring ways and her undeniable beauty, that he compared to his beloved magnolias, caused a longing in her heart.

Benjamin was elated when he received her reply a few days before the celebration at Atherton Hall. As he eagerly opened the envelope, the familiar scent of rose water on the stationary filled his senses as he anticipated being in her presence again in just a few short days. Sarah's feelings of admiration for him warmed his heart and her reassurance that all was well with her and her family helped to put him at ease.

Unknowing to her, Rebecca had also helped to keep Benjamin from worrying by keeping him busy with preparations for the upcoming celebration. She included Benjamin when choosing the menu for meals and recruited his assistance with the ordering of needed supplies from the local merchants in Atherton Village. While Rebecca managed the kitchen staff with the preparation of the food, Benjamin organized games and outdoor activities. On one of several trips to Atherton Village to pick up supplies that had been ordered, Rebecca suggested that Benjamin purchase a few extra sets of draughts to keep the children entertained. While he was in town, Benjamin also took the opportunity to hire a group of local musicians to play for the ball on the last night of their celebration.

Despite all the tasks that kept him busy during the days leading to the celebration, Benjamin found himself constantly thinking of Sarah. He wished this event, that under normal circumstances would be focused on the good fortune that he and his mother wanted to share with their friends, could be enjoyed without the worry of danger that could possibly face his and Sarah's families. However, Benjamin hoped this gathering would also serve as an opportunity for he and Sarah to discover the truth surrounding the mystery behind the deaths of his father and grandfather.

When Rebecca received a letter from both Caroline and Naomi Prescott confirming the day of their arrival, Benjamin was pleased to learn that the Prescotts and the Eldridges, along with Emma and Alexander, were due to arrive the day before the activities began. This would allow him to spend more time with Sarah. Benjamin also hoped that their early arrivals would give Sarah and himself more opportunities to seek answers to their questions and resolve their suspicions. He also thought that it would be easier for Sarah and himself to discuss their plan of action before the local guests from Atherton Village and the nearby farms arrived the following morning.

As Benjamin and Rebecca approached the coaches to greet their guests, Benjamin was immediately drawn to the black coach with the gold "E" emblazoned on the door. Rebecca politely waved as she passed by the Eldridge's coach to greet the Prescotts.

"Welcome to Atherton Hall!," Benjamin said as he approached the Eldridge's coach while Horace panted and wagged his tail as he stood beside him.

"Benjamin!," Lawrence called from the coach window.

"Glad to see you all had a safe journey," Benjamin replied as he reached to open the coach door to allow the ladies to exit first.

"Hello, Sarah," Benjamin warmly said as he offered his hand to help her from the coach while the two attempted to contain their excitement at the sight of one another.

"Horace!," Sarah said as the canine rushed toward her and pressed himself into the folds of her dress while she bent forward to scratch behind his ears and then stroked the fir along his back.

"Benjamin, we have been so looking forward to joining you and your mother for this wonderful celebration!," Caroline exclaimed as Benjamin turned to reach for her hand as she placed her foot on the ground as she exited the coach.

"We are so glad you all could join us!," Benjamin replied.

"Your home is lovely!," Emma exclaimed as she stepped out of the coach and looked upward to admire the brick mansion. "The magnolia trees are beautiful!," she continued while glancing at the two large trees on each side of the house.

"Yes, and my new trees along the path to the house are coming along nicely. They seem to be quickly growing with the passing days," Benjamin responded. "The saplings even had blooms on them a few weeks ago," he added.

"When we entered the iron gates, Sarah began to tell us how lovely they were in full bloom when she visited last month," Emma continued.

As soon as Lawrence and Alexander stepped out of the carriage, Horace suddenly stiffened when he saw Alexander. Alexander immediately jumped backwards as the canine slowly showed his teeth and began to growl.

"Horace, calm down, boy!," Benjamin said in an attempt to put the canine at ease when he saw the fear on Alexander's face. "I'm not sure what's the matter with him. He usually likes everyone," Benjamin continued while his suspicions about Alexander were reinforced as Horace began to obey his command.

"Hello, everyone!," James called out as Rebecca, Clarissa and his mother Naomi walked toward the Eldridge's coach after Rebecca greeted the Prescotts beside their coach.

"Rebecca!," Caroline exclaimed as she went to hug her friend. "Thank you for inviting us to this momentous occasion!," Caroline excitedly continued.

"We are so glad that you all could attend!," Rebecca replied while she gave Lawrence a hug. "It's a pleasure to meet you, Emma," Rebecca continued after Caroline made a quick introduction to her friend.

"Thank you for including me in this gathering," Emma politely replied. "Your home is beautiful!," she added.

"Thank you, Emma. We are glad you accepted our invitation," Rebecca responded. "Welcome, Alexander," Rebecca said as she looked directly into his eyes while trying to hide her animosity toward him.

"Thank you," Alexander replied in a monotone voice as he nodded his head while trying to avoid looking directly into Rebecca's eyes in an effort to hide his true feelings.

"It's nice to see you, Mrs. Prescott," Emma said as she turned to James's mother.

"Hello, dear," Naomi replied. "How are Patrick's parents?," she continued.

"I received a letter from Mrs. Adams not too long ago. She's doing as well as expected," Emma replied. "She is still having a hard time dealing with Patrick's death," she continued.

"I can certainly understand her grief. It is difficult to lose a child," Naomi sympathetically reflected. "I am looking forward to seeing them when they arrive tomorrow," she added.

"Please, everyone come into the house so we can get you all settled for your stay," Rebecca said as she began to lead the way toward the portico. "I'm sure you all would like to get settled after your long journey. Supper will be served in an hour," she continued as everyone walked toward the house.

"I'll have your coaches taken to the stables," Benjamin said as he motioned with his hand to two approaching servants. "While the horses are being attended to, I'll have your trunks delivered to your rooms," Benjamin continued while his servants welcomed the drivers of the two coaches and directed them to the stables.

"We have a full schedule over the next two days," Rebecca excitedly said. "More guests will be arriving tomorrow!," she added as they all approached the steps to the portico.

"We are so looking forward to the ball!," Clarissa pretentiously replied while she walked arm-in-arm with James as the memory of their introduction during a dance at Raleigh Tavern came to her mind.

"Benjamin has hired a fine group of musicians to entertain us!," Rebecca enthusiastically said.

Once they all entered the entrance hall, Emma and Clarissa immediately commented on the impressive interior architecture. Tula stood beside the newel post while she waited to assist Rebecca with escorting the guests to their rooms. As Tula began to walk up the stairs to lead the way, Rebecca reminded everyone that supper would be served shortly in the dining room.

After everyone took the brief opportunity to recover from their journey and become situated in their rooms, they returned to the dining room to enjoy a delicious meal. While everyone sat around the long mahogany pedestal table in the complementary Chippendale chairs and enjoyed the excellently prepared food, the women excitedly talked about their gowns for the ball while the men discussed the latest politics. When the leisurely meal had come to an end, everyone left the dining room to move into the front parlor for more conversation,

"Benjamin, how is the tobacco crop coming along?," Lawrence asked while everyone wandered into the front entrance hall toward the parlor.

"Very nicely! Atherton Plantation is going to have a good crop this year," Benjamin proudly said. "I am going to ride out to the fields early tomorrow morning. How would you like to join me?," Benjamin asked Lawrence.

"I'd like that," Lawrence answered before turning in the opposite direction as he was drawn into another conversation.

Benjamin took the opportunity to move closer to Sarah as they crossed the entrance hall.

"Let's find a place to talk in private," Benjamin prompted as he discreetly whispered in her ear.

"How will we get away?," Sarah asked in anticipation as the thought of being alone with him pleased her.

"I'll tell everyone I am going to show you the ballroom," Benjamin suggested while Sarah smiled and nodded as she realized it was a good plan.

After everyone was comfortably seated in the parlor and the conversation had restarted, Benjamin presented the idea to his mother and Sarah's parents and was happy when they all gave a nod of approval. As Benjamin and Sarah arose from their chairs, Tula entered the parlor carrying a tray containing a decanter of wine and lead crystal glasses.

"Thank you, Tula," Rebecca said as she watched Benjamin and Sarah disappear through the doorway.

"How was the journey to Atherton Hall? Did Alexander or Emma say anything out of the ordinary?," Benjamin asked as they strolled down the back part of the entrance hall.

"They were both quiet during most of the journey. Emma mostly talked about her excitement of seeing your home and some friends of Patrick's family," Sarah answered. "When Alexander did join the conversation, he talked mostly of himself and his accomplishments in the courtroom," Sarah sarcastically added. "His pompous attitude was a bit unnerving considering what he might be involved in."

"He certainly has a high opinion of himself," Benjamin replied.

"It's strange how someone with a large ego can have a distorted idea of the truth," Sarah responded. "I think I saw father discreetly roll his eyes when Alexander was bragging," she added.

"Yes, his dishonestly is quite obvious," Benjamin replied.

"I noticed that Horace did not take a liking to Alexander," Sarah said.

"Yes, I immediately noticed that," Benjamin replied as they continued down the hallway.

"They say that animals sense things," Sarah responded as Benjamin came to a stop in front of a set of double doors toward the back part of the house and reached for one of the doorknobs.

"After you, miss," Benjamin said as he opened the door and slightly bowed while motioning with his hand for her to enter first.

"Oh, how lovely!," Sarah said as she walked through the doorway and was immediately taken aback when her eyes scanned the room. "What a beautiful room!," she continued as Benjamin followed behind her.

"When I had the plans drawn up for the house, mother insisted she wanted a ballroom," Benjamin informed as he and Sarah both stood by the door and looked around the spacious room and then upward at the high ceiling. "When you and your parents visited last month the workers hadn't quite finished plastering the walls."

"Their craftmanship is quite impressive. I love how the doors open onto the terrace and overlook the gardens," Sarah admiringly said as she looked through the two sets of French doors while the afternoon sunlight cast a reflection across the wood floor. "And I'm sure the acoustics in here are wonderful!," she added while looking up at the high ceiling.

"Well, we will certainly be able to see if that is true the evening after next," Benjamin replied, referring to the upcoming ball. "Friends from Atherton Village tell me the group I have hired are excellent musicians," he continued.

"I know it is going to be a fine evening," Sarah responded.

"I have missed you since I last left Williamsburg," Benjamin confided as he turned to face her and looked deeply into Sarah's blue eyes.

"I received your letters," Sarah warmly replied as she returned his gaze. "They have been a comfort and made our distance seem short," she added.

"Whenever I look at those beautiful magnolia trees, they remind me of you," Benjamin affectionately said. "And our equal love for the beauty of nature," he added as a warm smile appeared on Sarah's face.

"It's a shame that all this natural beauty and what should be a pleasant weekend ahead is overshadowed by our suspicions," Sarah replied.

"We have to use this time, to see if we can find out more information from them," Benjamin said.

"The more we can get them to talk, the more they are bound to reveal some clues," Sarah responded.

"I agree. However, we have to be careful," Benjamin warned. "We can't forget about all the incidences where someone could have been killed," he continued.

"Yes, it frightens me to think about it!," Sarah replied with fear.

"Everything will be fine. We just have to be cautious," Benjamin empathetically said to ease her fears. "May I have this dance?," Benjamin playfully asked as he held out his hand in an attempt to lighten the mood.

"Well, of course you may, sir!," Sarah replied with a lighthearted laugh as she curtsied.

Unaware to both Benjamin and Sarah, one of the double doors to the ballroom slowly opened while the small crack between the doors allowed them to be unknowingly observed. The brown-haired female stood perfectly still as she peered through the small opening while she observed the happy couple as they relished in the joy of each other's company.

"If I may say so, you are a fine dancer, sir," Sarah said as Benjamin twirled her around.

"Thank you, miss," Benjamin said with a laugh while they playfully danced. "Mother said that dancing determines one's advantages in society. She made sure that I was schooled in the art as a young boy," he seriously said in a jest.

"Your mother and mine must have been schooled by the same book. When I was a young girl, I had lessons for a while from an instructor that visited our home. Mother basically told me the same thing," Sarah teased as Benjamin twirled her around and then came to a stop in front of him.

"Well, we can thank them both. If it wasn't for the wisdom of our wonderful mothers, we would not be here enjoying ourselves this very minute!," Benjamin playfully replied while they stood facing each other and laughing at their playfulness.

As their laughter began to subside and they both stood gazing into each other's eyes, Benjamin bent forward to kiss Sarah. Sparks ignited as their lips met and the two experienced physical intimacy for the first time. Warmth spread throughout their bodies and overcame their whole being as they experienced new feelings they both did not want to end. When Benjamin slowly pulled away, they stood perfectly still as they continued to stare deeply into each other's eyes.

"You know that you have captured my heart," Benjamin passionately declared.

"As you have mine," Sarah softly replied.

While the beautiful brunette with a fiendish smirk on her face watched the happy couple declare their love, her rage resurfaced as she recalled the pain and hardships their families had caused her. Although, her anger began to fade as she focused on her plan of revenge that was about to come true. She was confident her lover was going to make sure of that. What he didn't know was that he was about to take the fall for her evil deeds. She had no desire to leave the life of comfort that she had worked so hard to regain for a man that could never provide her with the social standing and material possessions she so strongly craved. She had become part of respectable society and had no plans of losing the financial security and the finer things in life that she was able to enjoy once again. A smug smile appeared across her face as she proudly acknowledged all her accomplishments. She was about to enjoy the rest of her life with a forgotten past and a secret that no one would ever discover.

As Simon Bartram's daughter quietly closed the door, she contently tiptoed down the hallway thinking her plan of revenge was about to come to pass.

Chapter 16

When Benjamin opened his eyes the following morning, the bright light he saw from his bed as he looked toward the windows was a welcome sight. During the night, a quickly passing storm with thunder and lightning had awakened him by surprise. The thunder and fierce lightning lit up the house as the heavy rain pounded the roof and the raindrops pelted the window panes. For a moment Benjamin hoped this wasn't a premonition of any danger that may lie ahead but quickly dismissed the thought since he always declared that he did not possess a single superstitious bone in his body. However, this morning Benjamin acknowledged to himself that he was relieved after he had gotten out of bed and peered out the window across the front lawn toward the river and realized the skies had cleared.

It couldn't be a more perfect day for outdoor activities. He welcomed the gentle breeze as it softly blew through the window and he heard the sound of rustling leaves on the magnolia trees. Benjamin hoped that the humidity would remain at a minimum so the day would be even more pleasant for everyone.

Once he dressed in his riding gear and ventured downstairs, Lawrence was waiting in the front entrance hall to accompany Benjamin into the fields to inspect the tobacco crop. Horace was patiently sitting by the front door and immediately stood on all fours and began to wag his tail when he saw Benjamin coming down the stairs. He and Lawrence had planned an early start in order to return to the house in plenty of time to welcome the many guests that were due to arrive by late morning.

When they approached the stables behind the house's dependency, a servant had Thunder and another horse saddled and ready for their ride.

"That's a fine-looking horse," Lawrence said as he assessed the white gelding while he and Benjamin stood outside the entrance to the stables.

"This is Lightning," Benjamin proudly replied as he softly rubbed the impressive horse's soft velvet muzzle.

"That's an intimidating name," Lawrence said with some concern as Lightning leaned his head downward to give Horace a nuzzle on the head.

"Despite his name, he is rather gentle," Benjamin informed to ease Lawrence's anxiety. "See, you have no reason to worry," he added just as Lightning gently nudged Lawrence's shoulder.

"I can see you are being truthful," Lawrence replied with a look of relief as he noted the animal's gentleness.

"He won't give you a bit of trouble," Benjamin reassured as he handed Lightning's reins to Lawrence.

"That was a fierce storm last night," Lawrence said as he placed his foot in the stirrup and mounted Lightning.

"Yes, it was a surprise. Although, the rain is good for the tobacco crop," Benjamin said as he settled himself into Thunder's saddle.

As they trotted down the path that led to the fields, Horace happily ran beside them before they eventually slowed the horses to a walk as they approached the tobacco fields.

"You do have an impressive plantation," Lawrence said as he looked out over the fields and then to the wooded areas beyond.

"Yes, my grandfather was granted a beautiful piece of property by King George I," Benjamin replied as he waved to a few of the workers in fields. "I'm sure that Penderley is just as impressive," Benjamin added.

"I would have to agree. Although, I am rather biased," Lawrence replied in a jest. "You will have to join us for a visit someday," Lawrence added.

"I'd like that," Benjamin replied while thinking the visit would mean spending more time with Sarah.

"It is true that both of our families have been very fortunate," Lawrence said. "And the future of our prosperity worries me with the political unrest," he added.

"What is the mood in Williamsburg?," Benjamin asked as he turned his head to look directly at Lawrence.

"With more Intolerable Acts being instituted during the first half of this year by the King, it is igniting some fierce discussion among lawmakers in Williamsburg. Unfortunately, Massachusetts is feeling the brunt of Britain's anger due to their involvement with the destruction of tea in the Boston Harbor this past December," Lawrence informed.

"It seems they are paying the price for their actions," Benjamin responded.

"And with a new Quartering Act, it is causing even more unrest," Lawrence said as he shifted in his saddle.

"I can see how it would be difficult to provide living quarters to a British soldier when you do not agree with Britain's treatment of the colonies," Benjamin pondered.

"We are living in trying times," Lawrence said. "I wonder how all this will end," he added while his eyes looked toward the horizon as if searching for the answer to his own question.

"It was obvious during supper last night that Alexander is quite pro-Britain," Benjamin recalled while he adjusted his hold on Thunder's reins.

"It is so hard for me not to lose my temper when I am around him," Lawrence replied while trying to contain his frustration. "He has such a high opinion of himself. And I can't imagine what Emma sees in a man like him," he continued as a frown appeared on his face.

"I have wondered about that myself," Benjamin replied. "Do you know much about Emma?," he asked.

"I know that Patrick Adams was her second husband. She was widowed once before Patrick. Both of her husbands died from accidents. It's strange they both had a similar fate," Lawrence answered.

"That is rather unusual," Benjamin replied as he recalled his and Sarah's suspicions. "How does Mrs. Eldridge feel about that?," Benjamin asked.

"Although Caroline has commented on it herself, I try not to say too much to her about that situation. She and Emma are friends and I don't want to cause any tension between us due to my dislike of Emma's choice of an escort," Lawrence explained.

"Certainly, she wouldn't be upset by your concern," Benjamin replied.

"Once you are married, you will understand," Lawrence said with a laugh.

"You are aware that I care very deeply for your daughter," Benjamin prompted as he reached to tenderly pat Thunder's neck.

"Yes, your interest is quite obvious to Caroline and me," Lawrence replied as he gave Benjamin a knowing look.

"I hope there are no objections," Benjamin optimistically responded.

"We do not disapprove of your interest in Sarah," Lawrence assured. "We were pleased when we first noticed your interest in her," he continued. "As you know, we have been friends of your parents for many years and we have such a high regard for your family," he added.

"Mother has expressed the same feelings," Benjamin replied. "I'm glad that no one objects. I have the utmost respect and admiration for Sarah," he assured.

"I believe that Sarah feels the same about you," Lawrence said as he noticed a look of contentment on Benjamin's face.

"I'm understanding then that you do not disapprove of me courting her with the hope of asking for her hand in marriage," Benjamin prompted.

"Such a union is what we have hoped for Sarah," Lawrence happily replied.

Having secured Lawrence's blessing and with a newfound feeling of contentment, Benjamin quickly changed the subject while they picked up their pace to ride deeper into the tobacco fields. Upon returning to the house after a pleasurable outing, they had just enough time to change and assist the ladies with final preparations before the guests began to arrive.

By late morning, a number of coaches began to enter the iron gates of Atherton Hall as the many local guests from Atherton Village and nearby farms came to join the festivities. The downstairs rooms of Atherton Hall were filled with mingling guests and the rumbling sound of voices. Refreshments had been laid out in the dining room for everyone to enjoy at their leisure. Earlier in the morning, the servants had set up several groups of tables and chairs in the shade of the magnolia trees on each side of the house to provide areas for relaxation and conversation.

During the early afternoon, a few groups of guests sat around each of the tables enjoying the soft breeze and a refreshing sip of a cool beverage as they engaged in cheerful conversation. Horace happily raced along the lawn playing with a group of children as they spun whirligigs on a string. An occasional cry of joy could be heard when a young child successfully scooped a ball into a cup or someone successfully played the wining move during a game of draughts. Frequent shouts of triumph echoed across the lawn while some of the older children happily played trap ball with their fathers.

Clarissa and James were returning from a stroll on the lawn as they approached a group of guests seated at one of the tables in the shade of the magnolia tree near the house. Emma was engaged in conversation with Penelope Baldwin while Alexander sat on her opposite side and impatiently waited for her attention. Naomi Prescott and Rebecca sat on the opposite side of the table and could be overheard laughing as they reminisced about the past.

"Did you two enjoy your stroll?," Naomi asked her son and daughter-in-law as they approached the table from the front lawn while arm-in-arm.

"It is an exceptionally pleasant day," James responded to his mother while Benjamin and Sarah approached the group from the front of the house.

"Are you two enjoying yourselves?," Rebecca joyfully interrupted while noticing the smiles on Benjamin and Sarah's faces.

"Yes, Mrs. Thompson. It's a lovely party," Sarah sweetly answered.

"Yes, James," Naomi continued. "It is a beautiful day! We couldn't have asked for better weather. Penelope, I don't believe you have met James's wife," Naomi announced as she turned to her friend. "Clarissa this is Penelope Baldwin," she continued with the introduction.

"Have we met before?," Penelope asked Clarissa as if she already knew her. "You do look awfully familiar," she continued as Clarissa attempted to hide her feeling of unease.

"I don't believe we have ever met before," Clarissa nervously responded as James noticed his wife's discomfort.

"I'm sure we have," Penelope bullishly insisted as she studied Clarissa's facial features. "It'll come to me eventually," Penelope adamantly continued while appearing deep in thought as she pondered her memory.

"I'm sure I would remember you if we had met before," Clarissa insisted.

"Georgeanna, is that you?," Penelope confidently asked Clarissa while both Emma and Alexander's eyes widened with shock.

"My name is Clarissa," Clarissa quickly answered.

"Are you sure? Well, you certainly resemble a girl I once met by the name of Georgeanna," Penelope rudely persisted while Sarah and Benjamin looked at each other after observing Emma and Alexander's reaction.

"You are obviously mistaken," Emma politely said to Penelope in an effort to defuse the tension.

"My memory never fails me," Penelope replied as she shook her head in disbelief.

"Well, it was certainly nice to meet you, Mrs. Baldwin," Clarissa sweetly said as she firmly guided James away from the table to continue their walk.

"Alexander, let's go into the house for some refreshment," Emma suggested after politely excusing herself and quickly arising from her chair to escape Penelope's overbearing personality and any further discussion of Clarissa.

"That's an excellent idea," Alexander happily agreed as he followed after her.

As both couples left the table, Sarah and Benjamin suspiciously looked at each other while they appeared to comfortably settle in two of newly vacated chairs. As they joined Rebecca, Naomi and Penelope in conversation, Sarah and Benjamin shared a secret laugh as they realized they both could still see the redness and frustration on Penelope's flushed face over her disbelief that her memory had failed her.

Later that afternoon, a beautiful brunette tensely leaned again the trunk of a stately magnolia tree nestled along the river's edge hidden from the view of Atherton Hall and its occupants. As she gazed out over the river, she was oblivious to the beauty of nature as several birds flew through the sky and the late afternoon sunlight reflected off the water. While deep in thought, the sound of approaching footsteps interrupted her anxious demeanor.

"I've missed you," he alluringly said as she turned her head to look at him after recognizing the familiar voice who had interrupted her thoughts. "I want to take you in my arms this very minute and make love to you," he seductively continued as he reached to take her in his arms.

"Yes, my darling, we will have plenty of time for that later," she replied as she pulled away while still pretending to share his enthusiasm. "Someone might see us," she reminded him.

"It's time we finished this," he said in frustration.

"Yes, I agree. And by tomorrow it will all be done," she replied in relief.

"Then we can move forward with our life together," he said with delight.

"I was just admiring this beautiful river. Wouldn't it be a shame if Sarah accidently fell in and drowned?," she wickedly asked. "Just think of the pain that Lawrence Eldridge would suffer," she added with an evil smile.

"That's an excellent idea," he replied. "We just have to find the right time," he added.

"We need to find an opportunity when that annoying Benjamin Thompson is not around," she angrily replied.

"We should easily be able to find an opportunity between now and tomorrow," he said to ease her anger.

"Just make sure there are no mistakes this time!," she said in frustration. "That old biddy almost blew Georgeanna's cover, didn't she?," she sarcastically added.

"Don't worry, my love, it will definitely be taken care of this time with no mistakes," he assured.

"And make sure you don't leave any clues that will make anyone suspect us," she specifically demanded.

As the immoral female seductively leaned back against the tree, he stood lusting after her beauty and her seductive figure. A wicked smile appeared across her face while she wallowed in the twisted joy of her evil thoughts and her power over him while he foolishly focused on the new life he thought they were about to share.

GARY ROWE

Chapter 17

The following morning, the household of Atherton Hall began with a slow start as its occupants recovered from the day before that had been filled with socializing and outdoor activities. However, the activity gradually increased for those preparing for the many local guests that would be returning for the formal ball later that evening. Rebecca met with the servants and made her final rounds in the cookhouse while Benjamin greeted the musicians who had arrived early to set up in the ballroom.

By late afternoon, local guests began to arrive as the coaches once again lined the pathway that led to Atherton Hall. The house was soon filled with elegant ladies and distinguished gentlemen dressed in their formal finery as they anticipated an evening of good food, conversation and dancing. Ladies were adorned in silk ballgowns, elegant hairstyles accentuated with pearls, ribbons and bows and sparkling jewelry at the neckline. Gentlemen were dressed in embroidered tailcoats, neatly powdered wigs and pristine white stockings. The elegant couples filled the ballroom as the musicians began to play and the dancing soon became underway.

Rebecca and Benjamin stood inside the doorway to the ballroom as they greeted their fashionably dressed guests. Benjamin tried not to appear distracted as he and his mother politely spoke to everyone as they entered while he inwardly anticipated the arrival of Sarah from her room upstairs. Benjamin was soon relieved when he saw Sarah and her parents appear in the doorway. After he and Rebecca exchanged a few niceties with Caroline and Lawrence, Benjamin focused his attention on Sarah.

"Sarah, you look lovely," Benjamin affectionately said as he admired her elegant appearance.

"Thank you, Benjamin. And you look just like the perfect gentleman," Sarah playfully returned the compliment as she assessed his neatly tailored clothes.

"May I have the first dance?," Benjamin asked Sarah as he held out his hand.

As they walked further into the ballroom and stood on the side of the room waiting for the next round of dancing to resume, Sarah and Benjamin began discussing their suspicions that were foremost on their mind.

"I still keep thinking about that incident yesterday with Mrs. Baldwin," Sarah recalled. "I wonder what it all meant? Whatever it was, it certainly caused tension among them," she added.

"I am convinced they are all connected in some way," Benjamin confidently replied as he noticed Emma, Alexander, Clarissa and James standing together on the other side of the room.

When the musicians brought the current round of dancing to an end and another round began, Benjamin led Sarah to the center of the ballroom floor as they happily joined a group to perform the minuet. Even though their thoughts were focused on the mystery that surrounded four particular guests, they were elated to see each other when the circle came around and they were rejoined as partners to continue down the line. As the dance came to an end, the happy couple glowed as they left the dance floor.

"Would you like some refreshment?," Benjamin asked Sarah while they walked away from the center of the room.

"Thank you, but I think I am going to mingle with Clarissa and James to see if I can discover more information," Sarah replied as she glanced at them across the room.

"I'll try and see what I can find out from Emma," Benjamin said when he noticed that Emma had left Alexander to speak with Mr. and Mrs. Adams. "Let's meet up once we've talked to each of them and see what we can piece together," Benjamin continued as they prepared to part ways. "Be careful!," he whispered before turning in the opposite direction.

"You too," Sarah affectionately replied with a smile before turning to leave.

As Sarah made her way across the room, she was silently trying to think of ways to discover more information.

"Hello, everyone," Sarah said as she approached Clarissa, James and Alexander standing beside the refreshment table. "Are you all having a good time?," she asked.

"What a grand evening!," Clarissa said as she looked around the room at the happy couples dressed in their finery while conversing and dancing.

"What a wonderful way to end this happy celebration," Sarah replied.

"Benjamin and his mother have overcome quite a bit of sadness and misfortune," James empathetically said. "I'm glad that life is better for them now," he added.

"Yes, life can have some unfortunate circumstances," Alexander said in a bitter tone.

"Where is Emma?," Sarah asked Alexander with feigned innocence.

"She's speaking to Mr. and Mrs. Adams," Alexander answered as he nodded in Emma's direction.

"I love your gown," Sarah said as she turned her attention toward Clarissa. "That is beautiful silk fabric and a lovely shade of green," she continued.

"Thank you, Sarah. James had it ordered specially for my dressmaker," Clarissa pretentiously replied. "It came from one of my favorite importers up north," she added.

"I remember hearing you say at mother's party that you and Emma were originally from the northern part of the Virginia Colony," Sarah prompted Clarissa. "Did you two grow up together?," she asked.

"No, we were not acquainted until after meeting here locally," Clarissa answered.

"Clarissa grew up in Alexandria," James said to Sarah. "Isn't that right, dear?," he prompted his wife.

"James, there is no need to bore Sarah with the details of my life," Clarissa teasingly said to James as a disguise to hide her annoyance.

"What brought you to southern Virginia?," Sarah asked Clarissa in an effort to get her to reveal more information.

"It just so happened that I met my second husband as he was returning from a business trip," Clarissa quickly answered as her annoyance grew.

"Why don't we all take a walk outside?," Alexander interrupted while sensing Clarissa's anger. "It's a pleasant evening with a nice breeze," he added. "A walk near the magnolia trees along the river's edge would be nice."

"That sounds like a wonderful idea. Ladies?," James asked.

"Oh, I think I'd like to dance," Clarissa said.

"There will be plenty of time for dancing. The evening is still young. Why don't we enjoy a little outdoors while it's still daylight outside," James persisted.

"James is right. We might as well take full advantage of the natural beauty that surrounds Atherton Hall while we are here," Alexander said to encourage everyone.

"It certainly is a beautiful place," Sarah said as she looked at Alexander and then Clarissa.

"I...," Clarissa began to protest as James took her by the arm to escort her outside while she turned her head to look at Alexander in confusion.

As the foursome left the ballroom and strolled through the main hall toward the front door, Clarissa wondered why Alexander Drake had suggested they go outside.

Back in the ballroom, Benjamin approached Emma after the elderly couple she was talking to had turned to leave. Emma remained standing alone deep in thought while appearing to listen to the musicians play and to watch the dancers in the center of the ballroom floor.

"Good evening, Emma," Benjamin said as he startled her.

"Benjamin!," Emma replied as her wandering mind was brought back to the present. "What a lovely evening!," Emma continued in an effort to hide her distraction.

"Where is Alexander? He should be put to shame for leaving such a beautiful girl unattended," Benjamin teased.

"I left him with Clarissa and James while I spoke to Mr. and Mrs. Adams," Emma answered.

"I'm sure they were glad to see you and comforted by your presence," Benjamin responded.

"Mr. and Mrs. Adams have had their share of sadness," Emma replied. "As we all do during our lives," Emma reflected.

"That is true. However, I believe the secret to happiness is how we deal with those sad times and overcome them," Benjamin replied.

"I have come to realize that as well," Emma responded.

"We must focus our energy on positive things!," Benjamin said to help lighten the mood.

"Enough talk about sadness!," Emma replied. "It certainly is a lovely ball. Thank you again for including me in such a grand affair," she continued in an effort to change the subject.

"It is my pleasure. I am so glad you are enjoying yourself," Benjamin replied.

"Your home is a wonderful place. Although, I have not had the opportunity to see your gardens," Emma replied as she looked through the French doors and across the terrace toward the garden wall.

"Let me take you on a tour," Benjamin offered while thinking this was a good opportunity to continue to learn more about her.

"That would be nice. And some fresh air would do me good," Emma said as Benjamin began to lead the way toward the French doors that opened onto the terrace.

As Benjamin and Emma exited the ballroom, Horace was comfortably resting on the terrace floor just outside the doorway and immediately arose when he saw Benjamin.

"Hello, boy!," Benjamin affectionately said to his beloved pet. "Would you like to join us on a tour of the gardens?," he playfully continued as the animal wagged his tail and eagerly turned to lead the way down the terrace steps.

"The gardens are absolutely beautiful," Emma said once they entered the garden gates and she began to admire the neatly shaped boxwoods set within the brick walkways and the colorful seasonal flowers that adorned the beds.

"My grandfather had a passion for nature. He looked at these gardens as his sanctuary," Benjamin replied. "He grew up in England and always admired the grand gardens of the English estates. He and my grandmother Elizabeth shared their passion for nature and they planned the gardens together during the construction of the original house," Benjamin explained.

"A beautiful garden certainly can make one forget their problems...at least temporarily," Emma replied.

"It's ironic that you say that. Grandfather once told me that the most difficult problems could be solved while sitting among the beauty of nature and enjoying the tranquility and peacefulness that nature provided. It allowed one to clear the mind and focus solely on the issue," Benjamin reflected.

"Your grandfather sounds like a wise man," Emma said.

"I think of him often when I visit the gardens. I recall seeing him many times from the upstairs windows while he peacefully sat on one of the garden benches," Benjamin responded while looking back toward the house. "Thankfully, the gardens were spared in the fire," he added.

"I was so sorry to hear of your loss," Emma said. "I can't imagine the pain that you and your mother have had to endure," she empathetically added.

"Thank you for your kind words," Benjamin said as he saw the genuine kindness in her eyes.

"Life can certainly be painful at times. However, I believe life is a gift from God and He gives us much joy also," she added in a caring tone.

"When you all arrived, I heard James's mother ask about Patrick Adams's mother," Benjamin prompted.

"When I was very young, I married an older man. We were not married very long when he unfortunately passed away," Emma said. "Then, a year later I met a man who was friends of his family and I married again," she continued. "It wasn't long before he tragically died in a fall," she added.

"Life can give us some difficult situations," Benjamin sympathetically replied.

"Yes, it never seems to work out as we plan. I never thought that I would have already married two times when just being shy of thirty years old," Emma said. "I almost feel as if people look at me in a strange way due to my unfortunate circumstances," she added.

"Well, you can't possibly hold yourself responsible for your husband's fates," Benjamin prompted, hoping for further disclosure.

"After being widowed the first time, I almost thought of returning to northern Virginia where I grew up," Emma said.

"It must have been difficult for you," Benjamin replied.

"It was very difficult. But then I met Patrick and he was so kind to me. He was my savior in a way," Emma responded. "I met Patrick when I was returning home from a visit with my parents up north. He was returning from a business trip. We were so happy and then his accident happened," she added.

"If I may ask, what happened to him?," Benjamin inquired.

"He was riding back from the fields one morning and was thrown from his horse," Emma emotionally answered as she tried to hide her pain.

"Emma, I hope you don't think I am being too forward with what I am about to say," Benjamin said as Emma inquisitively looked into his eyes. "You seem like a kind and caring person and I have to wonder what you would see in a man like Alexander," Benjamin continued. "He is surrounded by so much controversy."

"Benjamin, things aren't always as they appear," Emma replied.

"What do you mean?," Benjamin asked with growing curiosity.

"A few months ago, before I met Alexander, I was walking back to my shop one evening and I saw a man and a woman in an embrace in a nearby alley. At first, I didn't realize who the man was but when I took a second glance, I saw that it was Alexander. I couldn't forget what that lady looked like because I remember thinking that she ironically looked a lot like me. Fortunately, they did not see me," Emma explained.

"Who was the woman?," Benjamin asked.

"I didn't think much of the incident at the time but later I learned that woman was married to James Prescott," Emma answered.

"Oh, I see," Benjamin replied as a shock appeared on his face as he began to put the pieces together.

"I don't even know where to continue," Emma said as if her thoughts were in knots.

As Emma paused to gather her thoughts, Benjamin's mind was racing as he began to process this newly discovered information.

"I am sure you know of the infamous traitor Simon Bartram," Emma prompted.

"Yes, he is well-known throughout the colonies since his trial drew so much publicity," Benjamin replied while wondering if she was going to confess that she was Simon Bartram's daughter.

"My brother Francis was briefly married to that criminal's daughter," Emma bitterly said as she saw the look of shock appear on Benjamin's face.

"Really?," Benjamin asked while still in shock, even though he sensed she was telling the truth.

"My family was opposed to that union from the beginning and later learned that their suspicions were correct when they discovered she was indeed a woman of questionable morality," Emma explained. "That woman trapped my brother into marrying her with a web of lies. They were only married for a very short time and then he died under mysterious circumstances," she continued.

"That must have been difficult for you and your family," Benjamin sympathetically responded.

"My brother and I were very close when growing up even though I left home at a young age and moved to the southern part of Virginia to marry my first husband. When my family informed me of his death, it nearly devastated me," Emma continued as her revelations seem to lift a heavy weight off her mind.

"That must have been an awful time for you," Benjamin replied.

"Yes, it was. And it has haunted me ever since. I vowed to myself that I would one day find out the truth," Emma continued to explain.

"How did you come in contact with Alexander?," Benjamin asked.

"When I first moved to Williamsburg after Patrick died, I made several inquiries and I soon learned that Alexander was Simon Bartram's defense attorney during that trial. I assumed that he may be able to provide me with information that could lead me to Simon's daughter so I pretended to be interested in him," Emma continued to explain. "It wasn't long before I learned that Alexander is an awful man. I have been misleading him to find out information," she further explained. "When I first met Clarissa Prescott, it became obvious that she was the woman I saw him with in the alley and I initially thought they were just simply two people having an illicit affair.

But the more I learned about that trial and Alexander's association with that criminal's daughter, it became clear that it was a possibility Clarissa could be Simon Bartram's daughter," Emma concluded.

"If Clarissa is Simon Bartram's daughter, wouldn't she know who you were by your name? Surely, if you and your brother were close, he would have spoken about you to her," Benjamin stated.

"That's true, however my family always called me by my middle name," Emma explained. "I was born Emma Marie Beckham. Then yesterday, when you witnessed that exchange with Penelope Baldwin my suspicions were confirmed," she continued.

"How so?," Benjamin asked.

"My brother was married to Georgeanna Bartram," Emma revealed. "Mrs. Baldwin grew up with my mother and she and her late husband happened to be visiting the Beckham Estate soon after Francis and Georgeanna were first married. Later yesterday evening, Mrs. Baldwin insisted to me that she was the same woman who was married to my brother. Even though Georgeanna had improved on her appearance since then, Mrs. Baldwin still recognized her," Emma continued as she noted Benjamin's intense interest in what she was saying. "I also learned that your family as well as Sarah's has a connection to that trial and it is rumored that your families have no lost admiration toward Alexander," she continued.

"Both of our families have had strange 'accidents' happen over the last few years," Benjamin said. "I am now beginning to believe that he is definitely involved," he added.

"I have to apologize to both of your families for bringing that awful man back into their presence," Emma said.

"It must have been Clarissa who Sarah overheard talking to Alexander outside of your shop," Benjamin deducted out loud.

"What do you mean?," Emma asked in confusion.

"After the tragic fire that caused the death of my father and grandfather, I found a torn sleeve in the ashes the next morning accented with unique buttons. That confirmed that it wasn't an accident and that a stranger had been in the house when the fire started. Father revealed as much before he went back in the burning house to try and save grandfather. My suspicions about Alexander being a possible suspect regarding the deaths of my father and grandfather, first began the night of the Eldridge's supper party when we first met. I became suspicious of you also due to your association with Alexander and the similar buttons that you have for sale in your shop," Benjamin confessed.

"Poor James, he must have no idea what his wife is capable of," Emma confirmed.

"Are you sure he is not involved in this also?," Benjamin suspiciously inquired.

"I highly doubt that. I have talked to him quite a bit and he has never given me any reason to believe otherwise," Emma concluded. "He has no idea that he could be in danger since her second husband died in an identical circumstance as my brother," she continued.

"Oh, no!," Benjamin exclaimed as he realized Sarah was in danger.

As Benjamin and Emma stood staring at each other and processing all the information that had just been revealed, they both reached the same conclusion. There was no doubt that Clarissa was Simon Bartram's daughter and she and Alexander had obviously conspired to murder for their own vengeful purpose.

pleasant evening with a nice breeze," he added. "A walk near the magnolia trees along the river's edge would be nice."

"That sounds like a wonderful idea. Ladies?," James asked.

"Oh, I think I'd like to dance," Clarissa said.

"There will be plenty of time for dancing. The evening is still young. Why don't we enjoy a little outdoors while it's still daylight outside," James persisted.

"James is right. We might as well take full advantage of the natural beauty that surrounds Atherton Hall while we are here," Alexander said to encourage everyone.

"It certainly is a beautiful place," Sarah said as she looked at Alexander and then Clarissa.

"I...," Clarissa began to protest as James took her by the arm to escort her outside while she turned her head to look at Alexander in confusion.

As the foursome left the ballroom and strolled through the main hall toward the front door, Clarissa wondered why Alexander Drake had suggested they go outside.

Back in the ballroom, Benjamin approached Emma after the elderly couple she was talking to had turned to leave. Emma remained standing alone deep in thought while appearing to listen to the musicians play and to watch the dancers in the center of the ballroom floor.

"Good evening, Emma," Benjamin said as he startled her.

"Benjamin!," Emma replied as her wandering mind was brought back to the present. "What a lovely evening!," Emma continued in an effort to hide her distraction.

"Where is Alexander? He should be put to shame for leaving such a beautiful girl unattended," Benjamin teased.

"I left him with Clarissa and James while I spoke to Mr. and Mrs. Adams," Emma answered.

"I'm sure they were glad to see you and comforted by your presence," Benjamin responded.

"Mr. and Mrs. Adams have had their share of sadness," Emma replied. "As we all do during our lives," Emma reflected.

"That is true. However, I believe the secret to happiness is how we deal with those sad times and overcome them," Benjamin replied.

"I have come to realize that as well," Emma responded.

"We must focus our energy on positive things!," Benjamin said to help lighten the mood.

"Enough talk about sadness!," Emma replied. "It certainly is a lovely ball. Thank you again for including me in such a grand affair," she continued in an effort to change the subject.

"It is my pleasure. I am so glad you are enjoying yourself," Benjamin replied.

"Your home is a wonderful place. Although, I have not had the opportunity to see your gardens," Emma replied as she looked through the French doors and across the terrace toward the garden wall.

"Let me take you on a tour," Benjamin offered while thinking this was a good opportunity to continue to learn more about her.

"That would be nice. And some fresh air would do me good," Emma said as Benjamin began to lead the way toward the French doors that opened onto the terrace.

As Benjamin and Emma exited the ballroom, Horace was comfortably resting on the terrace floor just outside the doorway and immediately arose when he saw Benjamin.

"Hello, boy!," Benjamin affectionately said to his beloved pet. "Would you like to join us on a tour of the gardens?," he playfully continued as the animal wagged his tail and eagerly turned to lead the way down the terrace steps.

"Go find Sarah!," Benjamin said to Horace as the canine alertly looked upward towards Benjamin's face and then darted down the garden path toward the house.

Emma immediately reached down to raise the skirt of her ballgown with both hands as she and Benjamin raced through the gardens following behind Horace as he darted ahead of them. A fierce anger rose within Emma as she realized the time of retribution for her brother's death had finally arrived. Panic and fear consumed Benjamin as he realized that every second counted as he rushed to save the woman he loved.

When Horace reached the brick porch at the back entrance, he leaped over the steps and onto the brick platform and hovered near the door as he anxiously looked back at Benjamin.

"Let's split up," Benjamin suggested as he flung the door open to let Horace enter ahead of them into the back of the entrance hall.

"I'll go back to the ballroom and see if they are there," Emma said as they quickly entered the hallway.

"Okay, I'll check all the rooms along the hallway," Benjamin said as he and Horace rushed in the opposite direction.

While Benjamin and Horace hurriedly continued down the center hallway, Benjamin stopped at every doorway to look into each room. Becoming more worried when he did not find Sarah, he eventually heard several voices as he made his way closer to the front parlor.

"Mother, have you seen Sarah?," Benjamin frantically asked as he rushed to her when he saw her engaged in conversation with a group of guests.

"She was talking with Clarissa a short while ago in the ballroom," she answered. "Then I saw the two of them leave with Alexander and James," she continued.

"Where are they now?," Benjamin demanded.

"I overheard James suggesting the four of them take a walk down by the river," Rebecca answered. "What's the matter?," she asked in concern when she noticed the panic on her son's face.

"I'll explain later," Benjamin frantically answered as he quickly departed the room.

As Benjamin darted back into the front entrance hall to find Horace whining at the front door, Emma came rushing up behind them.

"They are somewhere outside!," Emma called to Benjamin as she approached him from behind. "Penelope Baldwin told me she saw them leave through the front door," Emma continued in a panic as she and Benjamin rushed toward the door.

Benjamin distraughtly reached for the doorknob as Horace impatiently rushed through the opening in the door and dived over the steps as he darted toward the river.

Chapter 18

"Benjamin does have an impressive estate," James said as he gazed toward the river in front of Atherton Hall while he and Clarissa strolled arm-in-arm across the front lawn.

"I understand that your plantation is as equally impressive," Sarah said to James while she and Alexander walked along beside them. "I hear that you have breathtaking views of the James River," she added while noticing a proud smile appear on James's face.

"Thank you, Sarah. Father was rather proud of his land. And, of course, its success. I want to be able to pass his legacy along to my own children someday," James replied. "Clarissa and I plan to have several children," he continued while fondly smiling at his wife and lightly squeezing her hand.

"James, please don't bore everyone with the details of our life," Clarissa teased as she purposely withdrew her hand from James's grasp in an attempt not to upset Alexander with talk of her and James's relationship.

Clarissa experienced an uneasy feeling as they continued across the lawn toward the river. She had carefully planned for Alexander to eliminate Sarah when no one else was around and this was not happening exactly as she had planned. Clarissa wondered again what Alexander was thinking when he had invited James and herself to join he and Sarah outside. She hoped for Alexander's sake this was not the time he chose to carry out their devious scheme of revenge. This time, Clarissa was determined that nothing was going to interfere with her plan. Once her plan was complete, Alexander would be left to take the blame while she lived a life of comfort and the high social standing she had worked so hard to achieve.

"I'm sure the thought of grandchildren makes your mother happy," Sarah said to James while Clarissa became more irritated as Sarah continued on a subject that could upset Alexander.

"It certainly does and she keeps asking me when we are going to bless her with our first," James replied as Clarissa winced.

"I love Benjamin's magnolia trees," Clarissa said in an effort to change the subject while she pointed to a nearby tree as they got closer to the river's edge.

"Yes, they are beautiful!," Sarah exclaimed as she and James left Clarissa and Alexander standing together while they continued toward the tree. "I love how the magnolia tree gives one the feeling of strength and permanency," she continued while looking upward at the majestic evergreen unaware of the danger that surrounded her.

"It is said they can live for centuries," James replied in a serious tone.

THE MAGNOLIAS OF ATHERTON HALL

"Why don't we all return to the house. I want to dance!," Clarissa interrupted as her feeling of unease grew.

"We have come to this spot to do exactly what has to be done," Alexander said out loud surprising Clarissa.

"What do you mean, Alexander?," James asked, noting his wife's discomfort.

"Yes, Alexander. Whatever do you mean?," Clarissa asked with feigned innocent.

"Would you like to tell them or should I?," Alexander authoritatively asked Clarissa while being confused by her response.

"I don't know what you are talking about!," Clarissa accused Alexander while noticing the uncertainty on James's face.

"Clarissa, what is this all about?," James asked with confusion.

"Enough of this! You know exactly what I'm talking about!," Alexander angrily insisted as he quickly pulled a concealed pistol from his side.

"What! What are you doing, Alexander?," Clarissa cried out in horror when she saw him pointing the pistol in the direction of Sarah and James.

"I'm doing exactly as we planned, Georgeanna," Alexander coolly replied. "Sarah will accidentally fall into the river and James will try and save her. Unfortunately, they will both drown in the process," Alexander calmly continued.

"Don't listen to him, darling!," Clarissa cried out to James. "He must be mad!," she exclaimed in an effort to save herself.

"What do you mean?," Alexander shouted. "This is what you have wanted for a long time!," he accused.

"He's crazy, James! Don't listen to him!," Clarissa pleaded.

"What are you talking about?," Alexander demanded. "You were just using James as part of your plan to take revenge on the Judge for your father's execution. Remember, we already eliminated the prosecutor John Thompson," he forcefully reminded Clarissa.

"Oh, my God!," Sarah screamed in horror. "Clarissa, you are Simon Bartram's daughter!"

As Sarah cried out the surprising revelation, James trembled in shock and disbelief as he glared at the woman he called his wife.

"Tell me this is not so!," James desperately asked, hoping this was all a case of mistaken identity.

Clarissa started to deny James's accusation, but could no longer bring herself to deny the truth when James looked directly into her eyes as if he could see right through her.

"Alexander, you don't want to do this," James said in a calm voice after turning his head toward Alexander while his reasoning began to outweigh his emotions.

"She just used you in her plan of revenge," Alexander shouted at James. "Just like all the rest!," Alexander revealed.

"Alexander, put the gun down," James continued in a slow even voice.

"The two of you move toward the river," Alexander forcefully demanded as he waved the barrel of the pistol at Sarah and James. "Georgeanna, you get over here by me!," Alexander demanded when he noticed she was slowly trying to move away from him.

"You fool!," Clarissa wildly retorted as she responded to her true name while reluctantly returning close by his side.

While Clarissa slowly moved toward Alexander, Sarah and James stood in fear as Alexander pointed the pistol directly at them. Suddenly, a faint voice could be heard calling out from across the lawn in the direction of the house.

"Sarah!," a familiar voice called. "Sarah!," the voice called again as it echoed in the distance.

As Alexander quickly turned to look back toward the house, James spontaneously grabbed Sarah by the arm as he quickly guided her in the direction of the large magnolia tree that stood nearby. A loud explosion sounded as flares of yellow and orange could be seen from the base of the pistol after Alexander turned back toward them and fired the weapon directly at Sarah. Sarah quickly fell toward the ground as she and James leaped behind the large tree. As the bullet loudly ricocheted off the trunk, pieces of bark flew in all directions.

Clarissa screamed when she turned to see Horace charging toward her and Alexander with an open jaw. As the protective canine took a giant leap toward his prey, his jaw latched onto Alexander's familiar wrist. The gun fell from Alexander's hand onto the grass as Horace began to ferociously bite his arm.

Alexander fell to the ground as he unsuccessfully tried to fight off the animal. Benjamin immediately darted in the direction of Sarah while Emma charged toward Clarissa. As Horace continued his attack, Alexander curled into a ball on the ground in an attempt to protect himself while the canine viciously mauled him.

In a last attempt to feign innocent, Clarissa intently reached for the pistol on the grass.

"Oh, no you don't!," Emma declared as she placed her foot over the pistol on the ground.

"Can you believe what that awful man tried to do to us?," Clarissa falsely accused Alexander in desperation, unaware of Emma's true identity.

"You lying witch!," Emma accused as she carefully threw the gun a safe distance away from Alexander and

Clarissa. "You killed my brother Francis!," Emma fiercely said as she savagely reached to grab Clarissa.

When Clarissa realized Emma's true identity, she undoubtedly knew her case was hopeless. Clarissa quickly raised her dress off the ground while she desperately darted in the opposite direction along the river's edge. Emma was close on Clarissa's heals when she reached to grab the bow tied at the back of Clarissa's waist but suddenly Clarissa faltered on the slippery incline. In a quick moment, Clarissa fell sideways into the marshy bank causing a huge splash as her body hit the muddy water close to the river's edge. The weight of her wet clothes began to pull her downward into the murky water as she struggled to stay afloat.

"I can't swim!," Clarissa called in desperation as she grabbed at a few tall weeds that grew along the riverbank.

"You feel helpless, don't you?," Emma goaded. "How does it feel to be at the mercy of someone else?," Emma said while continuing to taunt Clarissa. "How do you think my brother felt?," she continued as she thought about the pain her brother must have endured.

"Francis accidently fell down the stairs," Clarissa lied. "Help me!," she continued to call out.

"Are you sure that's what happened?," Emma continued while trying to draw a confession from her. "Tell me the truth or you will drown!," she threatened.

"Help me!," Clarissa gasped as she struggled to stay above the water while desperately clinging to the tall weeds.

"You don't deserve mercy!," Emma shouted while Clarissa's grip began to loosen on the weeds that she held onto for her life.

"Your brother had to die!," Clarissa screamed. "He had to be sacrificed!," she continued while justifying Francis's death in her mind.

THE MAGNOLIAS OF ATHERTON HALL

While Emma stared down at Clarissa in disbelief of her heartless confession, James and Benjamin suddenly appeared behind Emma on the riverbank. James placed his hands on each of Emma's shoulders as he gently guided her to the side while he and Benjamin bent down on the edge of the riverbank. The two men quickly pulled Clarissa out of the water as she gasped for air and reached for the safety of the riverbank.

As James and Benjamin guided Clarissa to her feet, the once elegantly dressed woman looked like a filthy mess with her disheveled muddy appearance and soaking wet clothes. Her neatly styled hair and elegant composure had disappeared and she no longer resembled the cool and collected individual she always portrayed.

"How could you do this?," James asked while still shocked at the unexpected revelation of who he truly married.

"Your father killed my father!," Clarissa shouted as she ignored James and turned her head to shout at Benjamin.

It took all of Benjamin's strength to contain his emotions while he gritted his teeth to refrain from harming her. James and Benjamin took Clarissa by each arm and led her back to the magnolia tree. Emma followed behind them in a daze while struggling to keep her emotions under control.

When they returned to the site of the confrontation, Emma was surprised to find Lawrence closely guarding Alexander with Alexander's pistol. She later learned that Rebecca had alerted Lawrence when Benjamin had appeared so distraught before he abruptly rushed out the front door. Emma felt no sympathy for Alexander as he sat demoralized on the ground wincing with pain while blood still ran down his arms staining the silk fabric of his tailcoat.

"You killed my father!," Clarissa yelled at Lawrence when she saw him standing over Alexander. "You fool, you ruined everything!," she continued while focusing her anger on Alexander.

"Shut up!," Emma said as she pushed Clarissa from behind and onto the ground beside Alexander.

While the two criminals sat dispirited and defeated, Sarah watched the surreal scene while she sat safely at the base of the magnolia tree with one arm wrapped around Horace. Benjamin quickly rejoined Sarah as he sat down by her side and placed his arm securely around her shoulder to warmly embrace her. As Emma gained control over her emotions, she slowly walked over to the distraught James and took his arm in an effort to comfort him. Lawrence breathed a sigh of relief, realizing the nightmare was finally over.

THE MAGNOLIAS OF ATHERTON HALL

Atherton County, Virginia

Late June, 1775

GARY ROWE

Chapter 19

The coach entered the iron gates from the main road and continued onto the pathway leading to Atherton Hall. The familiar lemony scent Sarah loved so much filled the air and overtook her senses. As she excitedly gazed out the window of the coach at the magnolia trees that lined the pathway, Sarah never could have imagined that less than a year after her first visit she would be returning not as a guest but to make Atherton Hall her home.

As the Eldridge's coach continued to travel down the pathway toward Atherton Hall, Sarah and her parents were silently absorbed in their own thoughts as they continued to gaze out the windows of the coach.

When Lawrence looked back inside the coach, the leather upholstery and shiny brass accents that adorned the luxurious interior, reminded him of the lifestyle that he and his family were blessed to enjoy but sometimes took for granted. While his thoughts wandered over the political unrest that had occurred during the past year, Lawrence wondered how these events would affect his family due to the uncertainty that reigned over the economic future of the colonies. When he turned his head to look back out the window, he realized that it was also a time of hope.

With the colonies continued desire for independence, The First Continental Congress had met in Philadelphia during September and October of the previous year shortly after the celebration at Atherton Hall. Representatives from all colonies, with the exception of Georgia, defined a core set of tasks to be carried out. All agreed that the King and Parliament must be made to understand the grievances of the colonies and the representatives must do everything possible to communicate these concerns to the population of America and to the rest of the world.

During their discussion in October of 1774, they adopted The Declaration and Resolves which was a statement in response to the Intolerable Acts passed by the British Parliament. The Declaration outlined colonial objections to these Acts, listed a colonial Bill of Rights and provided a list of specific grievances. In response to the Intolerable Acts, the representatives also adopted the Articles of Association which prohibited trade with Great Britain and created citizen committees throughout the colonies to enforce the act.

Lawrence recalled how word quickly traveled throughout the Virginia Colony when Patrick Henry, with George Washington and Thomas Jefferson in attendance, made a passionate speech to the Second Virginia Convention on March 23, 1775 at St. John's Church in Richmond. When Patrick Henry declared "Give me liberty, or give me death!", he was unaware at the time that his passionate plea would swing the balance in convincing the Convention to pass a resolution that would provide Virginia troops for the Revolutionary War.

On April 18th, Paul Revere, a blacksmith in Concord, Massachusetts, warned the New England colonists of the advancing British troops and the following day the Minutemen in Concord clashed with the British Army. As both sides eyed each other warily, not knowing what to expect, a shot buzzed through the morning air. It became known as "the shot heard around the world" signaling America's call for independence.

Due to these conflicts, The Second Continental Congress met in Philadelphia on May 10th to determine their action for dealing with British threats, manage the Colonial war effort and incrementally move toward independence.

In early June, due to the rising unrest in Williamsburg, Lord Dunmore fled the Governor's Palace for refuge in Norfolk in an effort to gather Loyalist supporters in Hampton Roads. On June 15th, after being nominated by John Adams of Massachusetts, the representatives of The Second Continental Congress named George Washington as Commander in Chief of the newly formed American army and the news quickly spread throughout the colonies.

While Lawrence reflected on the notable events of the previous year and wondered what the future held for the colonies and his family, Caroline noticed a look of seriousness on Lawrence's face when she turned her head to glance at her husband. She initially wondered if his thoughts were of the political turmoil which they frequently discussed or if their return to Atherton Hall reminded him of the traumatic events that had occurred almost a year ago. Caroline deeply hoped that his thoughts were not of Simon Bartram's evil daughter and her misguided accomplice.

The trials of Georgeanna Bartram and Alexander Drake had created the same notorious publicity as the Simon Bartram trial did years earlier. The notoriety of the trials was constantly kept alive by exaggerated articles published in *The Virginia Gazette*. When the final verdicts were reported, the outcome was of no surprise to anyone. Due to Alexander's admission with his involvement in the death of John Thompson and General Robert Atherton and after Georgeanna confessed to the murders of two husbands, they were both sentenced to death by hanging. As the events of this horrible time in their lives slipped deeper into the past, Caroline hoped that the memories of this awful ordeal would soon be forgotten.

Caroline's thoughts turned to joy as she began to focus on Sarah's happiness. She was gratefully indebted to her dear friend Emma for her timely revelation to Benjamin that had ultimately saved Caroline's family. That same gratitude was overwhelmingly extended to James Prescott for his quick thinking that saved Sarah's life as well as his own. Emma and James had supported and comforted each other in their time of grief and had formed a close bond as they recovered from the harrowing ordeal. Caroline was elated when they both accepted the invitation to attend Sarah and Benjamin's wedding ceremony.

When a smile suddenly appeared on Lawrence's face as he began to think of his loving wife and his daughter's newfound happiness, Caroline wondered what had caused his change in mood.

"I am a blessed man to have such a beautiful daughter and a lovely wife," Lawrence said as he affectionately looked at the two most important women in his life. "Sarah, I hope you know how much your mother and I wish nothing but happiness for you," he continued.

THE MAGNOLIAS OF ATHERTON HALL

"Yes, darling, you have found a good man in Benjamin," Caroline happily said.

"If you are half as lucky as your mother and I, you and Benjamin should have a wonderful life together," Lawrence said as he lovingly smiled at his wife and then turned his head to look back at his glowing daughter.

"I am very happy!," Sarah exclaimed while the carriage came to a stop in front of the portico.

As Benjamin rushed out the front door and down the steps, Sarah beamed with excitement when she saw the man she loved hurrying to greet the coach.

GARY ROWE

Chapter 20

"Remember when we were young you always said you were going to carry magnolias on your wedding day," Lucinda said as she admired Sarah holding her bridal bouquet while she fondly recalled their childhood.

"I did always say that, didn't I?," Sarah replied with a laugh as she raised the bouquet of magnolias to her nose to smell the wonderful scent and then turned to look at herself in the looking glass that hung on the wall of her bedchamber.

"And you also predicted that you would have them planted all around your house," Lucinda recalled as she stood behind Sarah and looked over her shoulder into the reflection. "It seems that both of your wishes came true," she fondly added.

"Yes, but a more important wish came true too," Sarah replied as she assessed her appearance in the looking glass.

"What is that?," Lucinda asked.

"I found a man who deeply loves me and who has a genuine appreciation for the beauty of nature as much as I do," Sarah joyfully acknowledged. "And we have the rest of our lives to share it together!," Sarah happily added.

"I am so glad the entire family could be here to celebrate this wonderful occasion," Lucinda replied.

"Yes! I would be disappointed if Aunt Lavinia, Uncle George and you and Philip were not here," Sarah said.

"I see that William and Ethan still love to tease us as they did when we were young," Lucinda joking said as she recalled their arrival with their wives and children the day before.

"They are lucky men. They were blessed with loving wives like Rachel and Hannah who put up with their mischievous behavior," Sarah said with a laugh as she turned to face her cousin. "And their children are growing up so fast!," she added. "I am so glad that Grandfather Nathaniel was able to travel with them even though his health is failing," Sarah continued.

"Martha and Thomas are so good to him," Lucinda replied. "He dearly loves his family and they wanted to make sure he came with them so he didn't miss out on this memorable moment in your life!," she added.

"We have been blessed with a wonderful family!," Sarah happily replied.

"I don't want to overshadow your day, but Philip and I are expecting!," Lucinda said as she placed her hand over her stomach and smiled at Sarah.

"Oh Lucinda! I am so happy for you!," Sarah exclaimed as she reached to hug her cousin.

"I hope you and Benjamin will be as happy as Philip and I," Lucinda affectionately replied.

"Benjamin makes me very happy!," Sarah exclaimed as an image of Benjamin's face appeared in her mind.

"You look beautiful!," Lucinda said as she admired Sarah's wedding gown. "Well, you don't want to keep Benjamin waiting!," she added as they both turned toward the bedchamber door.

When Sarah and Lucinda reached the top of the staircase on the second-floor landing, Lawrence was eagerly waiting at the bottom of the stairs.

"You are so beautiful! I can't believe my little girl is getting married," Lawrence said as Sarah descended the steps while Lucinda followed behind her holding up the train of her wedding gown.

"I will still see you and mother often," Sarah assured as she hugged her father after reaching the bottom of the stairs.

Lawrence took Sarah's arm and escorted her through the front door and onto the portico. Benjamin was overwhelmed by the lovely vision of his beautiful Sarah in her wedding dress. After Lawrence escorted Sarah down the aisle to hand to her Benjamin and then seated himself beside Caroline, Sarah and Benjamin looked deeply into each other's eyes as they exchanged vows under the wedding canopy on the lawn of Atherton Hall in front of family and friends on a bright and sunny day in late June.

As their wedding reception continued on the front lawn after the joyous ceremony, Sarah and Benjamin happily mingled among family and friends as they accepted good wishes and blessings for a lifetime of happiness.

"Would you mind if I stole my wife for a few minutes to myself?," Benjamin playfully teased as he reached to take Sarah's hand while she stood talking with Rebecca, Naomi, Emma and James who were seated at a table on the lawn.

"Ahh, to be in love!," James jokingly said with a smile as he looked fondly at Emma.

"You two enjoy yourselves!," Emma said as she returned James's smile and then warmly looked at Rebecca and Naomi while they watched the happy couple turn to leave.

"I hope they will always be as happy as they are today!," Rebecca said as Naomi nodded her head in agreement.

While Sarah and Benjamin strolled across the lawn, they joyfully watched the smiles and laughter of their family and friends as they celebrated this joyful occasion.

"I'm so glad all of our family and closest friends could join us on our special day," Sarah said as she observed the crowd spread out over the lawn.

"Hopefully that will be us in a few years," Benjamin teased Sarah as he watched Ethan and William playing with Michael, Myles and Phoebe on the grass.

Rachel and Hannah laughed as they watched their husbands and children during the memorable scene while Horace playfully circled them and then stopped to affectionately lick Phoebe across her cheek.

"Would you like many children?," Sarah asked while she noticed Benjamin watching her little cousins.

"Yes! At least a son to carry on the family name and a blonde haired blue-eyed daughter to remind me of you!," Benjamin playfully replied.

"Hopefully we will be blessed with more than two," Sarah returned his playfulness with a lighthearted laugh.

"Aren't the magnolia trees beautiful?," Benjamin asked as they continued toward the river while he glanced across the lawn at the trees.

"Yes, but it's always sad to see the last blooms fade," Sarah replied as she noticed the few remaining blossoms that could be seen on the trees. "However, it's a joy to look forward to their return next year," she added with a smile.

While Sarah and Benjamin strolled along the river's edge enjoying the beauty of nature on this memorable day, Benjamin's pace slowed when he realized they were near the spot where he and Sarah almost lost each other the previous year. As they stood beside the trunk of the tree, Benjamin turned to face Sarah.

"This magnolia tree in particular has a special meaning to me," Benjamin said as he laid his hand on the trunk of the tree.

"Why this one?," Sarah asked as she glanced at a large white blossom on a low hanging branch.

"This tree saved the woman I love," Benjamin affectionately said as his fingers touched the still visible mark that the bullet had left on the bark of the tree.

"This tree saved both of us," Sarah warmly replied as Benjamin reach upward to retrieve the beautiful blossom from the nearby branch.

As Benjamin presented the fragrant flower to his beloved wife, he warmly smiled while looking deeply into her eyes.

"Let this be a symbol of our love," Benjamin declared as he presented the beautiful magnolia blossom to Sarah. "Pure and true and forever blooming," he whispered before softly kissing her on the lips.

When Sarah and Benjamin turned to walk arm-in-arm back toward Atherton Hall, they were consumed by an overwhelming sense of happiness as they looked forward to the years to come.

GARY ROWE

"SARAH AND BENJAMIN"
BY
VIVIEN WILLIS

GARY ROWE

ABOUT THE AUTHOR

Gary Rowe is a native of Portsmouth, Virginia. His family lineage in Virginia dates back to the 1700s. Gary's interest in Virginia's history and his love of nature combine to make *The Magnolias of Atherton Hall* a delightful and informative read.

Educated with a degree in Business Administration and Marketing Management, he has had two successful careers in banking and the telecommunications industry.

From an early age, Gary had a deep appreciation and keen observation of nature, family and life's memorable events. These observations, combined with his creative imagination and great writing skills, make his storytelling real and intriguing. You will see through his eyes the true values of love and relationships as his characters come alive off the pages and into your heart.

GARY ROWE

Also by Gary Rowe

RUMORS RAN RAMPANT DURING WORLD WAR II that German ships were roaming the US Atlantic shores. There were ominous stories about sailors dropping anchor offshore during the night and rowing to the North Carolina beaches. An old fisherman provided them with supplies. Elizabeth Thompson always wondered whether the old fellow was ignorant of the Germans' true purpose or if he had a sinister motive of his own. Only the echoes of time know the real truth. But one act of absent-mindedness – a German knife left beside a campfire one summer night – sets in motion a story of love when events from the past determine consequences for the future.

Made in the USA
Columbia, SC
07 September 2018